FAIRYTALE

Anne Laurie H. Pierre

Anne Laurie H. Pierre
annelauriehpierre.org
Phone: (832)-869-8230
Email: annelauriepierre@yahoo.com

Ordering Information: Quantity sales. Special discounts are available on quantity purchases by corporations, associations, and others. For details, contact the publisher at the contact information above.

Printed in the United States of America.

Library of Congress Control Number   2018915320
   ISBN-13:   IngramSpark print format   978-1-7336148-0-1
                       IngramSpark ebook format 978-1-7336148-1-8
                             Draft2Digital 978-1-7336148-4-9

Rev. Date: 01/10/2019

I would like to thank my mom
and dad for always
supporting me.

PROLOGUE

July 2008. Meridian, Idaho

Today was a beautiful day, it was warm, a beautiful day to spend time with my best friend, and that was exactly what I was doing. Nate and I were in the park of our neighborhood, we were the only ones there. We were sitting on the grass, playing Backgammon. "Belle," Nate called me. *Belle* was the nickname he gave me for my name; *Rosabelle*. I looked up at him expectantly, "If I win, you owe me a kiss." I did a double take.

"Eww," I said, disgusted. Nate gave me a challenging look. "Fine. But if I win, you will do everything I demand for a week."

"Deal." We shook hands on it. We played and I lost. I looked up at Nate, he was actually cute--with perfect dark hair and gray eyes that tended to be blue on some days. Nate reached closer to me and the next thing I knew, we were kissing, it was wet. We broke away.

"Rosabelle," A voice called. I looked up to see my dad.

"Shit," was all that could come out of my mouth. Nate and I were secretly best friends for a year, we had met when we were just seven years old, and we have been sneaking off to see each other ever since. Why? Nate was mixed, his mom was a Protector, who was raped by a Vampire. My dad was a Wolf-Shifter and my mom was a Minder.

"Rosabelle, what are you doing with that filthy Vampire boy?"

"Half-Vampire, sir." Nate tried to defend himself. The next few things happened so fast: my dad yelled at Nate for being close to me, Nate's mom and the rest of his family came in and defended Nate, my mom came to defend my dad, somebody called the police on all of us, and the next thing I knew, we were moving to Oregon.

As my dad was about to take off, I looked through the window at Nate's porch, he was there. He smiled at me and mouthed three words.

'See you again.'

CHAPTER ONE

February 2017. Eugene, Oregon.

It has been nine years since we had moved, now my dad had things to do with the pack back in Idaho. So now, we were moving to Idaho Falls.

~~~

We finally arrived, my dad parked in front of the house, it was a gigantic house, the neighborhood was beautiful, houses were far apart from each other, except for one house that was twenty yards away from our new house. There were lots of trees, which I didn't like because lots of trees meant snakes.

I got out of the car, my mom already liked the place. "Rose, what do you think?" My mom asked me.

"It's okay." I simply said. With that, I went inside, upstairs, and claimed my bedroom. It was huge with a private bathroom, walking closet, huge french windows. There was already a bed, sofa, and a huge mirror. My dad came in, carrying boxes. He was smiling, obviously happy with the place. I started unpacking, organizing my new bedroom.

Just as I was done, I looked over at the window and saw a boy next door, sitting on his window sill, watching me. He had dark hair, I could not really determine his eyes, but based on his face texture, the way his body shape was, I knew he was beautiful.

A moment later, he simply got up and left his bedroom, leaving me aghast. Who was he and why was he so familiar?

~~~

Morning came, I got up, took a shower, got dressed, went downstairs, and ate breakfast. My mom grabbed an empty glass and water appeared. My mom was a Minder, Minders had all kinds of gifts; hers was water. "Do you want water?" My mom asked me.

"No thanks," I said and got up. I was ready to go to school.

"Have fun at school," my mom said and hugged me. I walked out of my house and saw him getting in his car. I pretended he was invisible until I got myself out of the driveway and on the way to school.

When I got to school, I checked myself in the mirror and I saw a dark skinned girl with dark chocolate brown hair and chocolate brown eyes staring back at me. I smiled at myself in the mirror, today was a new day.

I got out of the car, went inside the school building, to the counselor's office to get my schedule. I had four classes each day: Ap English, Calculus, Physics, Spanish 4. Those junior classes were too easy. I walked out of the office and went to my locker. "Hey, you--" someone shouted. I looked around to see a girl with green eyes and brown hair. "You're new, right?"

"Yeah."

"I'm Samantha." She introduced herself. She was a bit hyper, which I liked.

"I'm__" I started.

"Rosabelle Foureau," she finished. I stared at her in wonder. "I'm a Minder." She told me.

"What's your specialty?" I asked.

"Mind-Reader, duh." She said, smiling. I smiled back. She looked at me with curiosity. "What's yours?"

"Umm," I stuttered. "It hasn't come yet."

"Oh," She simply said. "It'll come, don't worry."

"I hope so." I said. Minders have always started developing their specialties at the age of fourteen, just like Wolf-Shifters started to change forms after puberty. I had my puberty at thirteen years old, I was currently seventeen and I have not been able to change forms nor have any specialties.

"No way!" Samantha started. "You're mixed." I stared at her aghast. "Sorry, I can't help myself. So, what do you have for first period?"

"Don't you know that already?" I asked.

"Yes, but I want to keep it casual...first impression." She said.

"Yeah, you kind of ruined that." She laughed at me, I smiled.

"Come on, you have English. So do I. Let's go, the bell is about to ring." We entered the class and sat together. People started filling in their seats, three minutes later, every seat was filled except for the one right next to me. Samantha kept looking at the doorway expectantly.

"Who are you waiting for?" I asked curiously.

"The really, extremely, irresistible, hot guy that sits in that open seat next to you."

"Well, does he like you?"

"What do I know?" She said, ignoring the question. That got me suspicious.

"Aren't you a Mind-Reader and all?" I asked. She looked at me.

"Fine," she said, "He finds me annoying, a bit too hyper...just like you, but you like my hyper side. He's also mixed, that's what got my attention in the first place."

"You like him?" I asked.

"He's mysterious and all hot, but no." She said. I stared at her.

"No." I repeated.

"Why would I like somebody who finds me annoying and too hyper?" She asked, giving me an obvious look. "Besides, he has a girlfriend." She said, nodding to the seat right next to the empty seat beside me.

There was a girl with blonde hair, she looked at me, she had blue eyes. "May I help you?" She asked in a mean tone. I looked away, Samantha had a disgusted look on her face.

"I really hate her," she whispered.

I responded, "I can see that." Just as the bell rang, the teacher came in. He looked young, he went straight to his desk. A moment later, a boy walked in. He was broad, tall, had dark hair. He looked around the class, he had gray eyes. Why did he look so familiar?

"Nate Florus, you're late." The teacher said.

Nate was the boy who was my best friend for a year, we would sneak out to play with each other, he was the one I had my first kiss with. *Nate.* "Shit," I whispered under my breath. It was like he heard me, he looked at me. Of course, he heard, he was half-Vampire. We exchanged gaze, all of the secrets we've shared were laying right in front of us.

"Sorry, I won't be late again." Nate said, still looking at me. He walked across the room, sat on the empty seat that was next to me. I quickly looked away.

"We have a new student here today." The teacher announced, looking at me. "Want to come up and present yourself?"

I nodded, unsure. I got up, feeling Nate's gaze on my back. I faced the class. "I'm Rosabelle Foureau," I said. Nate's eyes softened, he was remembering me. "I used to live in Meridian, Idaho before I moved to Eugene, Oregon. Now, I'm back in Idaho." I looked at the teacher. "That's it," I said and went to my seat.

Throughout the rest of the class, Nate ignored me. After English, I had Calculus, it was fine for me since I loved solving. After that, I had lunch. As soon as I got my food,

Samantha came to me and guided me to a table where there was a cute, dark haired, green eyes boy sitting. "I'm Dylan." He said, smiling up at me.

"I'm Rosabelle." I replied back.

"Okay, enough with the introduction. Rosabelle, we have to talk." Samantha started.

"What about?" I asked, confused.

"Your first kiss." I went to a state of shock.

"You just met the girl and you're asking her about her first kiss," Dylan asked in shock.

She glanced at him, "If you knew who she had her first kiss with, you would have questions--" Samantha stated. Dylan got curious.

"Who?" He asked.

"Nate Florus." Samantha answered.

Dylan half-screamed, "What?" My eyes landed on Nate, he was staring at his food, his left ear was perched to one side and I knew he was listening to us. I tapped Samantha and thought. 'He's listening to us.' She gave me a nod, telling me that she knew. "Wait, I'm confused--" Dylan started saying "--you just moved here."

"Well, apparently, she used to live in Meridian and moved to Oregon." Samantha explained for me. "Rosabelle, I have a question for you--" I stared at her "--how was it?" I laughed at that.

"Umm," I stuttered, "I don't know."

"Come on!" Samantha complained.

"Fine, it was kind of we__." I said and they laughed. I glanced over at Nate and saw him smiling, trying not to laugh.

"Well, did you like it?" Samantha asked. Nate was still listening.

"Oh, my Gosh. Seriously?" I asked in disbelief. They both gazed at me. "I was eight, how was I supposed to know if I liked it or not?"

"Okay, you're right." Dylan said. "But now that you're seventeen, would you kiss him again?" I quickly looked at Nate and found him looking right back at me. I quickly looked away. Thank God I was black for I could not blush.

"Let's talk about something else, shall we?" I suggested.

"Come on, I know you want to talk about it." Samantha said.

I changed the subject, "Dylan, I can't seem to figure you out."

"What can't you figure out?" He asked.

"You are definitely not ordinary," I stated.

"I'm a Seeker," Dylan filled me in. That made sense. A Seeker was someone who was human, but knew and studied the Supernaturals. Seekers could define them by just looking at them. "You are so far a Minder, your body still has not formed the Wolf shape."

"Excuse you, but I haven't had my specialty yet, you're wrong." I informed him.

He argued, "I am a Seeker. I know when someone is a Supernatural and you are a Minder, you've already had your specialty, you just don't know what it is yet." He informed me. Samantha and I both stared at him.

I asked, "Well then, What is my specialty?" He simply stared. "I know that you know, it's part of being a Seeker."

"Yes, I do know, but I can't tell you. You have to figure it out."

"Come on, Dylan. Just tell her." Samantha said.

I was waiting. Dylan looked at me. "Sorry, I can't. It's part of the Seeker law." Seekers had this whole law about not telling Minders their specialties until they had everything figured out.

I rolled my eyes and looked at Samantha. "Tell me," I demanded.

"He's blocking me out," she said--obviously unsatisfied with not being able to read Dylan's mind.

"The funny thing is, you've been doing your specialty for three years." Dylan confirmed. I thought hard.

Three years ago, I started having an interest in drawing. "Drawing," I said in disbelief. "Are you fucking kidding me?" Samantha asked him if he was being serious, Dylan said nothing. At the corner of my eyes, I saw Nate laughing. "Why is this asshole laughing?" I asked loud enough for him to hear. He quickly looked at me, I gave him a smirk. He smiled and waved at me. Now I was surprised. Just like that, he got up and left the room.

"Did he actually wave at you?" Samantha asked in disbelief.

"He's mocking me." I said, pissed.

"I don't think he was." Dylan said.

"Yeah, he totally was. He thinks your specialty is a joke." Samantha admitted. "Something to be embarrassed about." I wanted nothing more than to go home and cry on my mom's shoulders. "Rosabelle, If I were you, I would be proud. I mean the world would be an ugly place without art in it--" Samantha said to make me feel better.

"The fact is, the world is already an ugly place." I said.

"But, it would have been uglier," she commented. I smiled, she was actually making me feel better. "I mean, Nate is cruel, he is the most popular guy at school, and let's not forget, he's an asshole__" I cracked up.

"I wonder what he would do if he heard you calling him that." I wondered, smiling.

"Oh, I know--" Samantha said, giving me the best impression of Nate. I laughed harder. "Oh, my Gosh. I love your laugh." Samantha told me.

"Thank you." I beamed.

~~~

Physics and Spanish were fun, I had to present myself. When the bell rang, I went to my locker to get my things and headed myself to the parking lot. Nate was standing next to my car, kissing his blonde girlfriend. "Excuse me," I excused myself. The girlfriend looked pissed. Sheesh.

I opened the car's door, aware of them watching me. "Hey, new girl--" She called me. I looked up expectantly "--this is my parking spot, I park next to my boyfriend's. I glanced at the car next to mine and it was Nate's. For some reason, the idea of me meeting Nate in the parking lot was quite satisfying.

"Sorry, but until I see it's a private parking lot with your name on it, I could really care less about it." I said, facing her. Her face twitched, she glared at me. I started to feel some sort of sensation in my brain.

"Tessa." Nate warned and the sensation was gone. I got into my car and ignored them. I drove out of the parking lot, glanced at them, they were kissing again. 'Wow,' I thought, rolling my eyes.

At home, dad was in his office, mom was reading in her room. She saw me, closed the book, and followed me to the bedroom. "So, how was school?" She asked me, sitting on my bed.

"Cool." I said.

"Did you make any friends?"

"Of course, mom. I'm not a freak." I said, rolling my eyes.

"Are they nice?"

"Yes, Dylan is a Seeker and Samantha is a Mind-Reader."

"Grandma was a Mind-Reader." My mom said. I nodded. She had a curious look on her face. "This Dylan kid, did he say anything about your specialty." I looked at my mom. She was excited and nervous.

I just could not tell her, she would have been so disappointed. "No, mom." I said. She looked at me quizzically. "Seekers aren't supposed to tell you until you know," I said truthfully. She still didn't quite believe me.

"Rosie, you know you can tell me anything." My mom called me Rosie. Dang, this was exactly what I did not want.

"Mom, I'm such a disappointment."

"Oh, Rosie. Why would you say such thing?" My mom asked, worried.

"Mom, my specialty is drawing," The room went silent, I was holding my breath. My mom was staring at me, her mouth gaped open, I was still holding my breath. The door opened.

"Dinner's here," my dad said happily, clearly not feeling the tension that was building.

"We'll be right down, Lucien__" My mom assured him. My dad left, "shall we go?" She asked. I nodded.

At dinner, my dad was chatting about his time with the Wolf-Shifters, he looked so happy. "So, Rose--" my dad called on me "--I was thinking of you coming to spend time with the pack and me on Friday, after school." I smiled. I've never seen the pack and I was super excited.

"I would love to." I said, excitedly.

After dinner, dad and my mom did the dishes. I went back to my room and did my homework. Shortly after I did my homework, I headed back downstairs. My dad and my mom were having a discussion. "Anne, I think you're over exaggerating--" my dad was saying "--drawing takes a lot of talent and specialty."

"Drawing specialty is for ordinary humans, not Minders." My mom said, her voice hushed.

"I've seen Rose's drawings and they are breathtaking, she can change the world with her drawings. Maybe that's her specialty."

"No Minder in this world has had a specialty in drawing. EVER." My mom said, reasoning with him.

"Anne, the world is screaming for a change." My dad said.

"Oh, my Gosh. For God's sake, Lucien--" My mom half-yelled "--no daughter of mine will have a specialty in drawing," I gasped. Tears sprang from my eyes. There was a sudden silence and the next thing I knew, both my mom and dad were standing in front of me. Of course, my dad probably sniffed me out and heard me gasp.

The doorbell rang, not one of us made a move to get it. I brushed away my tears and opened the door. I came face to face with Nate and his mom. I gazed at them confused, 'why are they standing on my porch?' "Hello, Rosabelle." Nate's mom voice was pleasant and welcoming. My mom and dad came behind me and stopped dead in their tracks. My mom and Nate's mom were glaring at each other, and my dad was glaring at Nate. Of course, it was no surprise.

Minders and Protectors were natural enemies as were Wolf-Shifters and Vampires. But Nate on the other hand, didn't care about that, being my best friend once and now dating Tessa, who was a Minder. "What has brought you here, Linda?" My mom asked, not bothering to hide her disgust.

"May we come in, it's a bit cold outside." Linda said, shivering. My parents just stood there, glaring at them.

"Sure, come in." I said, stepping out of the way. They came in, I closed the door.

"Nice home," Linda said, approving our home.

"Just cut to the chase, why are you really here?" My mom demanded.

"I wanted to invite you to dinner, Thursday night."

"No, thank you." My mom said abruptly.

"Mom," I warned.

She looked at me and sighed "what time?" She asked.

"Seven o'clock." Linda responded.

"We'll be there," I said. My parents looked at me suddenly. I simply shrugged.

"If you two don't mind, I wanted to talk to you about something." Linda said.

My parents looked at me without certainty. "Well, I'm going to go watch TV." I said. "Nate, wanna join me?" My breath was in my throat. He stared at me for a second and nodded.

~~~

Nate and I were sitting on the couch, watching Empire. "I'm sorry," Nate suddenly said. I looked at him. "That you are ordinary, that must be hard for your parents."

"I'm not ordinary."

"Yes, you are. Having a specialty in drawing is a total joke, tons of humans are gifted in art." He said. I felt my blood rushing.

"I am not ordinary." I said once again, convincing myself.

"Sure, whatever you say--" he added "--why are you back?" He gazed at me. Gosh, his eyes were so intimidating.

"Am I not allowed to be back? Last time I checked, I wasn't on an exile from Idaho." I said sarcastically.

"I see you still have a thing for a sarcasm," he smirked at me.

"I see you still have a thing for interrogating people," I smirked back.

"Oh, really." Nate started.

"Yes." I said.

"Nate, we're going," His mom interrupted.

"I'll walk you to the door," I said.

~~~

I woke up this morning, more relaxed than yesterday. I took a warm shower, got dressed, fixed my hair. I went downstairs, ate breakfast and went back upstairs to brush my teeth. I found it ridiculous when people brushed their teeth before breakfast. I applied some lip gloss. I didn't wear any makeup except for lip gloss. I believed that natural beauty was more beautiful than making up your face with makeup.

At school, I parked my car at the exact spot I parked it yesterday. I didn't give a worth about Tessa. I had the freedom to park wherever I wanted to.

Nate was already in his seat when Samantha and I walked into English class. He glared at me until I sat down. "Do you have to glare at me?" I asked him. Samantha was watching us.

"Why did you park in the exact same spot today?" He asked. Samantha smirked.

I gave him a look--"Geez, you really have a thing for interrogating people, don't you?"

"Aren't you the sassy one?"

"I'm proud," I said and Samantha laughed.

"You do know that Tessa is going to get back at you, right?" He said. There was careness in his eyes.

"Nice to know you care." I said.

"BITCH." I heard someone yell__Tessa. She marched down toward me, a moment later, her face was on my face. "Didn't I make myself clear when I told you to not park in my parking spot?"

"Didn't I make myself clear that until I see your name printed there, I will park as I desire?" I stood up to her, there were gasps in the air.

"I don't care about what you said, you are invading my space!" She shouted.

"Well, right now, you are invading my space--" I said back.

"Ooh," Some classmates cheered. She gave them a quick glance.

"If it weren't for those ordinaries here, your brain would be on fire--" She whispered quietly to me "--dumb girl."

"I'm actually very clever."

"No, you're not. If you were, you would know that I'm not the person that you would want to get on the wrong side of." She gazed icily at me.

"I'm not scared of you," I said defiantly.

"You should be."

"Rosabelle has the right to park wherever she wants to," Samantha defended me. I smiled.

"Mind your business, bozo."

"I would, but you see, Rosabelle is my business, so yeah."

"Back off," Tessa growled at her.

"I'm not afraid," Samantha said back.

Tessa warned, "You should unless you want to repeat last month's coincidence."
Samantha was blushing with anger, she suddenly got up and faced her with a glare. I
shrunk down in my seat. Nate was grinning, he was amused.

"No, you should be the one afraid." Samantha said.

"Why is that?" Tessa challenged.

"I know things about you that nobody else knows."

"Prove it."

"You are NOT a virgin, you lost it to your cousin last year on Halloween, which was
three months ago and you were still dating Nate." Everyone gasped in the room, there
were some kids in the hallway, watching.

"H-how d-did you know that?" Tessa asked. She was pale. I smiled, I knew Samantha was
a Mind-Reader.

"I have my sources," Samantha simply said.

"Everyone who is not in my class, OUT!" The teacher announced. Lots of students got
out. Wow, what a scene I have caused just because of a parking lot.'

"We are finally becoming popular," Samantha gleamed beside me.

~~~

Just like Samantha predicted, we became popular, everyone could not stop talking about
this morning. At lunch, Nate was nowhere to be found. School ended, I was walking in
the parking lot when I saw Nate leaning against my car. I stopped cold, the way his body

was leaning, him keeping a straight face, it was just hot, he was beautiful. "Were you waiting for me?" I asked him.

"I wanted to talk to you."

"Save me the speech of '*I should not park here.*'" I said.

"I just don't want her to hurt you." He said. I looked at him and he actually cared.

"I'm not the one she hurt," I said truthfully. He gazed at me. "I'm sorry." He simply nodded. "Did you two break up?" I asked and regretted asking right away. I needed to keep my mouth shut sometimes. He shook his head at me, why was he still with her? "Why?"

"Why not?"

She cheated on him, she had SEX with her own cousin, "Oh, I don't know. Maybe because she was having sex with her own cousin, that is so disgusting." I said. His jaw clenched.

"That is not your business, besides, I'm fine."

"Fine, did you know the most common lie people say is 'I'm fine?'" I stated. "You are not fine, I know you."

"You know nothing about me." Nate hissed at me. "We may have been best friends years ago and shared our first kiss with each other, but get your facts straight, you know nothing, so you just need to back off, and mind your damn business. What's between me and Tessa is MY business, not yours." I was shocked. He was glaring down at me. I could feel my blood rushing through my face. Thank God I was black, for he could not see me blush.

"I'm sorry," I simply said--turning away from him. I got into my car and drove away.

~~~

Thursday came, I was ready to go to Nate's house and have a formal dinner. Nate and I have kept our distances from each other, Samantha already knew what happened between us.

My dad was the one to knock on the door and Nate was the one to open it. He gazed straight at me before turning his gaze on my parents. "Mr., Mrs. Foureau." He nodded at me. "Welcome." My parents and I stood still for a moment before entering the Florus' house.

CHAPTER TWO

Dinner was quiet, too quiet. We all kept glancing at each other, none of us were eating except for me who was digging at my food. I was in my own little world that I didn't notice everyone was watching me. Linda was looking appreciatively at me, for me being the only one at the table to eat dinner. My parents were looking at me like I was crazy, Nate had a half-smile on his face. "Did you like dinner?" Linda asked expectantly.

I smiled at her, "I loved it, thank you." Again, the table was soundless, we were glancing at each other, none of us wanted to start a conversation. "Does this dinner have to be so awkward?" I asked out loud. Everyone looked at me.

"I'm going to my room, I have better things to do." Nate said, getting up.

"Why don't you show Rosabelle your room?" Linda asked in a demanding tone. Nate glanced at me for a moment, I glanced back, he made an acknowledgement with his head that I should follow him.

~~~

Nate's room was spacious, the walls were pure white. Like my room, he had a walking closet and a private bathroom. There was a desk in the room, when I passed by it, I saw a picture, my breath was caught in my throat. The picture was of us, his mom was the one who took it. We were eight years old back then, our arms were around each other, we were smiling at the camera. "You still have that picture," I said in disbelief.

"It's not like I have a choice, you made me promise to put the picture somewhere I would see it every day so that I could never forget about you." I laughed, remembering me making him take a vow.

"You didn't have to, that was years ago."

"I never break my promises, Rosabelle. I always keep my word, you know that." He said.

"I thought I didn't know anything about you--" I said, surprisingly with so much bitter.

"Don't start," he simply said.

"You never apologized for your reaction on Tuesday," I said.

"I don't have to, you were out of line and you pissed me off."

"I pissed you off or did your sluttly-bitchy girlfriend cheating on you with her own cousin pissed you off," I said truthfully.

"Get out," He simply said. I looked at him in disbelief.

"Gladly," I said. As I opened the door, I faced him once again. "You are right, I know nothing about you. You've changed so much and not in a good way. I can't believe I had my first kiss with you, you are not special. And one more thing, you can burn that picture of us." Before I closed the door, he was looking at me with so much hurt in his face.

I ran downstairs, opened the front door. "DAD, MOM. LET'S GO!!" I yelled loudly before dashing out of the front door.

I ran to my house, upstairs to my bedroom. I got out my drawing journal and started drawing. I wasn't paying attention at all to what I was drawing. I just drew and drew whatever my mind was willing me to draw. Just as I was putting my drawing journal away, my mom and dad walked into my room. "Rosabelle, what happened?" My dad asked, concerned.

"Nothing, he's a total douche bag, no, scratch that, he's an asshole."

"Aren't all Vampires assholes?" My dad asked. A moment later, we all laughed.

~~~

On Friday, my dad drove me to school because later he would pick me up so I could meet his pack. "I've been waiting for lunch so Dylan would know the details," Samantha said as she flopped herself down beside Dylan.

"What's going on?" Dylan asked, interested.

"Nate seems pissed today, Rosabelle, don't you think?" Samantha started. I rolled my eyes.

"I noticed that today, he told Mr. Sanchez to F himself."

"I heard." Samantha said casually. "Do you know the reason behind him being pissed off?"

"No, tell me." Dylan demanded.

"It's all Rosabelle's doing, my dear." Samantha commented.

"I did nothing wrong," I defended myself.

"Did you know you hurt his feelings?" Samantha asked me and I did not respond. She gazed at Dylan, "She told him that she should have never had her first kiss with him, that he isn't special--" Dylan gasped in shock, Samantha continued "--and that he should burn the only picture he has of the two of them together."

"I don't give a worth about his feelings, he's too aggressive." I admitted. I could feel Nate's gaze on me, I ignored him.

~~~

My dad picked me up after school. When we arrived, a whole lot of people greeted us, which I assumed was the pack. They were so much fun, awesome, telling each other jokes, goofing around. "Rosabelle, wanna shift with us?" A girl named Tia asked.

"I haven't shape-shifted yet." I said.

"You still haven't gotten your puberty?" She asked. I could feel my blood rushing through my veins.

"Yes, I'm just late."

"Yeah, it happens."

"Does it hurt the first time?" I asked, interested.

"You have no idea," Tia said. "It's like your bones are snapping, breaking in half, your body is twisting, you are in a terrible souffrance, and the terrible part is that the process is so slow the first four times, it makes it more endurable. After those four times, you change faster and it doesn't hurt. The more you shift, the less painful it will be."

"Gosh, I'm scared for my four times." I admitted.

"Don't be, you can control your shifting except for those fours. They are uncontrollable, the slightest anger, rage, could lead you to shift."

"Can you shift for me?" I asked, super excited. I have never seen a Wolf-Shifter transform before.

"Sure," she said__ "Hey, everybody. Our second leader wants to see us shift." Just like that, they were shifting one by one.

I gasped, they were so tall and big, they were not normal sized wolves. It was like if you were 6 feet tall human, you were going to be six feet tall Wolf. It was simply remarkable and breathtaking. My dad was smiling at my expression. "How cool is that?" My dad asked me.

"I have no words."I replied, gaping. My dad chuckled.

"I know."

~~~

We were driving in our neighborhood when I thought of something Tia had said. "Dad, what did Tia mean when she called me 'second leader'?" I asked, interested.

"Well, I am the leader of the pack and since you are my daughter, my heir, my blood...you are next." I nodded, but I was a bit confused.

"Wait, aren't Werewolves' leaders supposed to be Werewolves?" I asked the obvious question.

"It doesn't matter if you are half." My dad said.

"I know, dad, but I haven't shape-shifted yet or had any symptoms of becoming a Shape-Shifter." My dad grinned a little. "What?"

"It's just people have stopped calling us 'Shape-Shifters' and prefer the term 'Werewolves.' It's not like we turn every full moon with no control."

"Dad," I said in a serious tone.

"Don't worry, you'll shift one day--" my dad said assuringly.

"Well, what if I don't."

"You will."

"No, dad. Don't you get it? If I were to shape-shift, I would have done that already by now or at least I would have gotten the symptoms, but none of that has happened, so yeah, I'm freaking ordinary__" I yelled angrily. My dad parked in front of the house. I saw Nate on his porch, reading a book. I never knew he read books, then again, I knew nothing about him. My dad and I were still sitting in the car.

"You just need an inspiration." My dad said.

"No, dad. I don't need an inspiration. I just need to accept the fact that I'm ordinary. Is that why you brought me to see your pack, to have an inspiration. Well, it didn't work, did it?" I got out of the car, my dad followed.

"Rose__" He started.

"Don't 'Rose' me, dad--" I yelled "--I'm sorry that I'm not the daughter you wanted, that I'm such a disappointment." With that, I ran as fast as I could. I kept running and running, I heard close footsteps behind, trying to keep up. Assuming it was my dad, I ran faster. "Leave me alone." I yelled.

"Stop!" A voice responded. It wasn't my dad's. I turned around and saw gray eyes blazing at me...Nate. "Jesus, you are quite fast for an ordinary."

"Thank you--" I said, not meaning it "--what do you want?"

"I just wanted to make sure that you were okay," he said. I felt fire burned through me.

"Since when do you care if I'm okay."

"Since I met you." He said. I looked at him, he was being honest.

"You feel pity for me, my dad is pitying me also."

"I'm not sure your dad is pitying you, it's more like disappointed in you. I can't imagine being you right now." I felt my blood rushed through my face.

"I can't believe you right now," I suddenly yelled at him. He stood still, wide-eyed at me. "Who do you think you are to tell me what my dad is thinking about me? You know, you are such a hypocrite."

"Oh, hypocrite. Me?" He asked as if he could not believe what he just heard.

"Yes, you. You're like, don't get into your business, to mind my own business and just back off. and here you are, totally getting into MY BUSINESS."

"I, I." He stuttered. "I just wanted to know how you were doing and tell you how I see it."

"Oh, my Gosh. Would you look at that, it sounds exactly like what I was doing in the school parking lot on Tuesday and in your bedroom. Don't you think?" I said. We stared at each other for several seconds.

"I'm sorry." He finally said. A moment later, he was gone, leaving me breathless.

CHAPTER THREE

Saturday came, I stayed home, did my homework, studied, watched TV, played the piano and viola. Sunday came, and it was actually warm outside.

I sat on the porch, my drawing journal on my lap. Something suddenly hit me and I drew, everything became blurry as I drew.

When I finished, a car came into view and parked in the Florus' grass. The door opened and Tessa got out. As soon as she saw me, she gave me a smirk. I simply stared at her. A moment later, Nate was out of his house, he strode himself toward Tessa, and kissed her. I could not help but notice that he was not into it, he was not into her.

I could not help myself from smiling. Like he could sense my smile, he turned and gazed right at me. I gazed right back into his gray eyes that looked blue today. My heart was pumping faster and louder than usual, my breathing was abnormal. I was sure that he could hear the difference about me because he smiled---a knowing smile.

~~~

Monday came, I parked my car at the usual spot, Samantha and Dylan were waiting for me at my locker. "Hey, guys. What's going on?" I asked them. Samantha nodded off to a direction. I looked at the direction and saw Nate and Tessa arguing. Some kids stopped to watch them as well. "What are they arguing about?" I asked, curious. Samantha and Dylan looked at me with a smile on their faces.

"You." Dylan said. I went cold.

"What, what do you mean '*me?*'" I asked, shocked.

"Well, she was saying every trashy thing she could think about you and that just pissed him off, he defended you and told her off." I could not believe it. Suddenly, they stopped arguing, Tessa turned to look at me, so did Nate. Samantha, Dylan and I looked back at her. Suddenly I fell to my knees, my head was burning, it was like my brain was on fire. I clutched my head, nothing I could do could make it stop.

Tears sprang from my eyes. Suddenly the pain stopped and Nate was at my side, helping me get back on my feet. Everything around me was blurry, I could not see clearly or hear or even talk.

I noticed that Nate was carrying me somewhere, he laid me down on a soft surface and I knew I was in the nurse's office. I heard them talking, but I could not make out what they were saying. A pair of cool hands was on my head and the pain was fading until there was no longer pain.

I could see clearly now, both Samantha and Dylan looked angry, they were mumbling something about Tessa, Nate looked concerned for my care. I eyed the nurse weirdly. How did she make the pain stop? A second later, I knew she was special in healing. "How are you feeling?" She asked.

"Great--" I said, "--thank you."

"Okay, you are good to go, but make sure you have plenty of rest tonight okay." I nodded.

Samantha, Nate and I headed to English. "Thank you," I said to Nate.

"What are friends for?" He murmured half to himself.

~~~

Tuesday came, I was in English, listening to the teacher talking. "So you will have an assignment with partners, I will pair you guys up, don't expect to be pair with the person next to you or someone you talk to a lot."

Samantha murmured to me, "I knew it, but I was hoping he would have changed his mind."

Tessa was paired with a guy named Cody, Samantha with a girl named Britney. "Nate Florus, you are with Rosabelle Foureau." I stopped breathing. I could not help the excitement I was feeling of working with Nate.

"You'll write facts about each other and then, you'll write an essay about Supernaturals and what you think about them."

"Why Supernaturals?" Tessa asked.

"Because I believe they are real," the teacher said, matter of factly.

"Well, if you believe they are real, why don't YOU do your own research?"

"I'm gathering facts," the teacher said. I looked at Samantha, who was no doubt reading his mind. She gazed at me and mouthed the word. 'Crazy.' I felt a little relieved.

"By making us do your own work for you," Tessa sounded angry. Nate was watching her carefully.

"I'm sorry, but I'm the teacher here, and when I give you an essay, I expect you to do it." Silence followed. "Now, where were we?"

~~~

Samantha, Dylan and I were walking in the parking lot when I saw a group of people surrounding my car. "What's going on?" I asked, pushing myself through the crowd.

"Oh, my God. Who would do this?" Dylan asked.

"Tessa," Samantha said with disgust. My car was wrecked, there were paintings, the windows were all smashed, there were big letters on top of that--BITCH.

Tessa was grinning at me, I wanted to cry, but that would have given her the satisfaction. Nate came and stopped when he saw my car. Right away, his eyes landed on Tessa, they were icy cold, Tessa's grin faded. Nate walked toward her. I could not hear what they were saying. I walked away from my car, I had to walk all the way home. Samantha and Dylan started following me. "Rosabelle, wait up!" Someone yelled after me. Nate was running toward me.

"What?" I asked him.

"I'm sorry."

"Whatever."

"Are you okay?"

"No, your psychotic, bitch girlfriend wrecked my car. I am not okay."

"I'll give you a ride," Nate offered.

"I don't want your ride, I can walk home."

"Come on, Rosabelle."

"Clearly she doesn't want a ride with you. She can take the bus with me and Samantha--" Dylan said.

Nate glared at him. "Clearly I wasn't asking you for help," he responded back. There was tension between them. "I'll give you a ride." Nate insisted. I kept staring at him. "The Rosabelle I know would not let her have it." I felt a spark fly through me. I took hold of his hand and we walked hand in hand to his car. He opened the passenger door for me, everyone was watching us. Tessa had a shock expression on her face. I smiled maliciously at her.

Nate was driving when I thanked him. "You're welcome--" he said, glancing at me sideways, I smiled shyly at him. There was a red light, he stopped the car, looked at me. "Are you okay?" He asked for the second time. I looked at him and noticed his lips. I wanted nothing more than to kiss those lips. He reached up and touched my neck. I stopped breathing. "Your heartbeat is really fast," he said. There was hunger in his eyes.

"Have you ever tasted blood?"

"Besides my own, no." He said, "there are consequences if I drink anyone's or any animal's blood." We were driving again.

"What consequences?"

"If I drink, I will become a Vampire."

"What about Supernaturals?"

"I'll still be me."

"That's not so bad," I said. He half-smiled at me. I had an important question I needed to ask him. "So, have you ever been thirsty?"

"Haven't you?" He switched the question around, smiling a beautiful smile. I smiled back.

"I meant, have you ever been thirsty for blood?" He stopped short.

"I've only been thirsty for one person's blood," he said--looking straight ahead.

"Whose?" I asked, curious.

He looked at me for a moment, his face was serious. "Yours," he responded. I stopped breathing. "Don't worry, it's never going to happen, I don't have a dream of becoming a full-time Vampire."

"What are you talking about? I'm a Shape-Shifter and a Minder." He looked ridiculously at me.

"Yeah, who has not shifted into a Wolf yet and has an ordinary talent."

"Well, that's upsetting--" I said. We were quiet for the rest of the ride. "Thanks for the ride." I thanked him when he pulled up on his driveway.

"It's nothing." We both got out of the car together. "Can we start doing the project on Thursday?" Nate asked, looking at me carefully.

"Yeah, whatever." I simply said.

The door of his house opened and a young man in his early twenties walked out. "Hey, cousin. What's up?" He asked and eyed me. "You have a new girlfriend? You didn't tell me she was black." I gasped at his comment.

"Gee, aren't you still yourself, Edward?" I said, remembering his name.

"Hey, I know you...Rose, right?"

"Rosabelle." I corrected.

"So I guess you're not a new girlfriend." I simply stared at him, he patted Nate on the back. "Where's your girlfriend, I was looking forward to seeing her again."

"I don't have a girlfriend," Nate said carefully. I stared at him.

"What do you mean you don't have a girlfriend?"

"I broke up with her."

"Why?"

"Because she's mean, she's not my type." Nate simply answered. He was a bit uncomfortable.

"I thought bad girls were your type." Edward commented.

"Obviously you thought wrong." William looked at me and back at Nate.

"Well, I'm gonna go." I said. I started walking away.

"I'll give you a ride tomorrow?" Nate asked with a hopeful look on his face.

"Sure," I shrugged--walking away.

~~~

My parents were furious when I told them about my car, I had to practically beg them to let it go. My mom was taking care of the car business. I told my dad that Nate was the one who gave me a ride home and I was riding with him again in the morning. Even though my dad didn't like Nate, I could see that he was thankful of him. He told me that he would get Tia to give me a ride home.

Later that night, my mom came into my room. "I was thinking of getting you a new car." She said. I looked up at her in shock.

"Why? I don't want a new car." I stated. My mom had a shock expression across her face.

"Okay, well the mechanic said he will be done fixing your car in three weeks exact." I nodded, looking at her. "I'm sorry," my mom suddenly blurted out.

"Why are you sorry?" I asked, a bit confused.

"That you have to go through this."

"It's only making me stronger," I said truthfully.

"That's my girl," my mom smiled.

~~~

The doorbell rang, I raced to open the door. It was Nate. He smiled. "Ready?" He asked. I nodded, smiling.

We drove to school, listening to music. Nate and I pretty much had the same taste in music.

When we arrived in the school's parking lot, I saw Tessa's car was parked in the original spot I've been using. I simply rolled my eyes. Nate parked his car in his spot, he gave me a smile, and we both got out. There were gasps from Tessa and her little friends and a few kids. I smiled proudly, Nate seemed to be waiting for me. We walked together all the way to English.

I had Spanish 4 for fourth period, we weren't doing anything. I was having difficulty on what to draw when a wave of sensation went through me and I was sketching...fast. The bell rang, I closed my drawing journal and walked to my locker.

I closed my locker and smashed myself against Nate, my things fell on the ground. I was picking up my things when I noticed Nate checking my drawings. "Did you drew these?" He asked.

"Yes." I said, taking my drawing journal back. I got up and started walking away, he followed me. We were outside in the parking lot, I was searching for Tia.

"Those drawings--" he started, I looked up at him.

"Rosabelle," someone interrupted. It was Tia, she came over to us, glaring at Nate. Nate glared back, I smiled at her. "Ready to go?" She asked me, still glaring at Nate.

"Yes." I said. I looked at Nate, "I'll see you later, okay. Come to my place." He nodded and watched me go.

~~~

The doorbell rang, it was Nate. We went up to my bedroom, leaving the door half open. He sat on the mini couch that was in my bedroom and we started doing the tasks about us. We asked each other questions about the other, but we found ourselves answering them in a questioning form. Every time we got it right, we would find each other smiling. When we were done for the day, we just sat, doing nothing. He was looking around the room, thinking deeply about something. "I know what your specialty is," Nate suddenly blurted out. I rolled my eyes.

"Yeah, because I told you."

"It's not drawing," he said. I looked blankly at him.

"Then what is it?"

"Can I see your drawings again?" He asked, serious. I sighed and gave him my drawing journal. He looked through them. "Look, this drawing is you on the floor because Tessa used her specialty on you, this is your wrecked car, this is of me watching you through the window when you first got here, this is me and Tessa breaking up, and this is the last drawing, of me being in your room, your drawing journal in my hands, and you peering over my shoulders--like you are doing now." I gasped. My hands covered my mouth.

I never knew I've been drawing all those things. I just could not believe it, but I knew. I just knew, they were my drawings and they were telling me something. "I'm a Seer," I whispered.

CHAPTER FOUR

"You are a Minder after all," Nate said--smiling.

"I'm not ordinary," I said in disbelief. "I can't wait to tell my dad and mom." I could not wait to see their faces.

"They'll really be proud." Nate said. Suddenly, I grabbed him and hugged him with such force. After a moment, he hugged me back.

"Thank you," I whispered.

"What for?"

"For showing me who I am."

"Of course." He said after a moment, "you're welcome." There was a sudden cough in the room, I looked up and saw my mom. I ran and hugged her.

"Whoah." My mom said, confused. "Rosie, are you okay?"

"I'm more than okay, mom." I unhugged her. I handed her my drawing journal. She looked through them and looked back at me. "I'm a Seer, I have visions, I can see the future." Tears started springing from her eyes. She was happy and proud.

"Oh, my God." She gasped. "I knew you weren't ordinary, I just knew it."

"If it wasn't for Nate, I would not know I was a Seer."

"Thank you," My mom thanked him.

"Seriously, it was nothing--" Nate replied, but he was obviously pleased with himself. "Well, um, I'm gonna go." Nate said, a bit awkwardly. I smiled at him.

"Yeah, we'll finish tomorrow?"

"Yeah, see you."

At dinner, we told my dad about my specialty, he was happy with a hopeful look in his eyes, but there was a tiny hint of sadness. I knew it was because I didn't shape-shift into a Wolf yet, he just had big hopes for me, and I could not help myself from feeling that I have disappointed him, but that wasn't an option. I was going to find the inspiration that I was going to need to shape-shift into a Wolf.

~~~

For the next few days, Nate and I spent a lot of time together, he drove me to school and home, we met each other at our lockers, we spent time in each other's houses. Sometimes, he would come and sit with Samantha, Dylan, and I at lunch. Tessa always gave me cold glares. "Come on, Rosabelle. Can't you see what that bitch is up to?" Samantha asked me.

I had told her about my specialty. Dylan already knew about everything. No surprise there, he was a Seeker. "I can't, it doesn't work that way."

"It actually kind of does," Dylan said. "You just need to focus." I closed my eyes and tried to focus on Tessa, nothing came.

"Here, take my hand, now try." Dylan held my hand, I tried again.

"Still nothing."

"Try it on me," Samantha was eager, I tried again.

"Nope, nothing's happening."

"What are you guys doing?" A voice came from behind me, it was Nate.

"We are trying to trigger some future out of her," Dylan explained.

"Also what your psycho ex-girlfriend is up to in the future," Samantha added.

"Can't you figure it out, you're a Mind-Reader and all--" I said.

"Wait, you're a Mind-Reader?" Nate said, a little nervous.

"You look nervous," I said to him.

"I wonder why?" Samantha wondered and received a glare from Nate. "Anyway, I can't. I can only see through people's past, present and what future plans they are thinking of. But, as we know, Tessa is the only one to know about what she wants in the future."

"So, you have no idea what she's going to do?" Dylan asked.

"Well, I do know for sure that she is plotting some kind of revenge for Rosabelle, but I can't seem to find out--" she glanced at me "--so get to work."

"Okay, fine." I rolled my eyes. "Nate, give me your hands." He did as he was told. I focused on him with all I could. "This is not working." After a moment, I got out my pencil and drawing journal. "Maybe this could help." I wrote my name and the date on the bottom of a new page, nothing happened. "I give up." I said.

"It'll come to you." Nate assured. He put his hand on my shoulder and suddenly, it all started happening and my hand flew across the page.

Moments later, I closed the journal, gasping for air. Everyone at the table was looking at me in awe. "See, it worked." Dylan smiled.

"Let's see what you drew." Samantha demanded. I opened it and came across the drawing. We all stared at it speechless, unable to say anything. It was Nate and Tessa on his front porch...kissing.

"I have not spoken to her since we broke up."

"Well, you sure will do more than speaking to her in the future." Dylan said.

~~~

Nate and I were in my dad's study room, we were doing ordinary's research on Supernaturals, we were both working. He was researching and doing the essay while I was working on the poster. I could write beautifully in cursive and my drawings were spectacular. "I believe our presentation will be the best," Nate said quietly.

"Of course, who could beat my awesome drawings and cursive writing--" I said, smiling proudly.

"I could." Nate said, smiling back. I laughed.

"You wish."

There was a gentle knock on the door, my mom walked in. "Here are your Chinese meals." My mom handed us what we ordered.

"Thank you, Mrs. Foureau." Nate thanked my mom, she smiled genuinely.

"You're welcome." My mom was staring at the poster. "The Supernaturals?"

"Well, our teacher is apparently a nerdy geek, he believes we exist." I said.

"Ordinaries, can you blame them?" I guess not. "Well, I'm gonna go and pick up some groceries." My mom said and left.

"I was thinking since we have not seen each other for nine years--" Nate started "--we should hang out outside of school and each other's houses."

Spending time with Nate sounded exciting. I was really looking forward to it. "Yeah, it will be fun to catch up." I said. He smiled approvingly at me.

"How about tomorrow?" He asked. "It's Friday, after all."

"Yeah, works for me."

~~~

Friday came, our project was due today and it was the best by far. At lunch, Samantha, Nate, Dylan, and I were in the library, reading a marvel. After school, Nate waited for me besides his car. Tessa was giving me icy stares. "Ignore her, because we're about to have fun." Nate said excitedly.

Nate and I had fun, we went to the amusement park, goofed around. we went on the sky flyer and roller coasters. I screamed my head off that I literally damaged my vocal chords...literally. "What time is it?" I asked Nate.

"10:07," he responded. We were eating popcorn candy.

"I have to be home by midnight."

"Or else your dad will have the pack searching for you," he joked and I laughed.

"He actually would."

Nate drove me home, we gave each other jokes, talked, etc. "I had fun today," Nate said. We were on his driveway.

"Me too, thanks for today."

"You're welcome. We'll pick up again tomorrow?" He asked. I nodded smiling. "It's 11:59."

"Oh right. Bye." I said and walked away.

"Right on time." My dad said as soon as I opened the door.

"Hey, dad."

"Did you and Nate have fun?"

"Yeah, lots."

"Will you be here tomorrow?"

"No, Nate and I are going to hang tomorrow." My mom came out of nowhere.

"Are you two dating now?"

"No, mom. Just catching up on the nine years we've lost."

"I'm glad."

"Well, if you'll excuse me, I'm pretty much tired and tomorrow is a big day." I said.

~~~

Morning came, Nate talked me into taking a walk with him in the woods. "Are there snakes out here?" I asked. He looked at me with a serious face.

"No," He lied.

"Are you sure?"

"Yes." His face was more serious.

"You're lying."

"How do you know if I'm lying?" He challenged me.

"You always have a serious face on when you're lying." I said. He stood there, shocked.

"There are only few."

"Good, because I hate snakes."

"How come?"

"Snakes are evil, sneaky little demons." He suddenly laughed at me. "Seriously, in the Bible, Satan turned into a snake. In Harry Potter, Voldemort's pet was a snake. There is something about snakes that I just do not like. They freak me out and they look way too freaky and weird...I mean with their flat heads and split tongues...HEESH,"

"So you hate snakes." He had an amused look on his face.

"Aren't you the one who's afraid of clowns." I was smiling.

"Dude, they are creepy, with those colorful hair and big red nose. The have a huge smile on their faces and they keep watching you, not making a sound."

"Does your mom still do the annual costume party?"

"Yeah."

"Good," I said with a huge smile on my face. He watched me suspiciously.

"Don't even think about it," he said. I looked at him innocently.

"What?"

"Okay, two can play that game, come." I followed him.

I asked him, "So, how did you and Tessa meet?" He kept walking.

"First high school Halloween party, we got drunk and we hooked up." He acknowledged.

"But, you're still a virgin, right?" I asked. My breath caught in my throat.

"Why would you assume that?" He asked. I questioned myself a little.

"I don't know, are you?" I asked. He looked at me with a smirk on his face.

"Are you?" He turned the question back to me.

"Why would you assume that?" I quoted the question back at him. He laughed, shaking his head. "Yes, I am still a virgin." I said with a proud look on my face.

"Really." He asked, shocked. "Why do you have this proud look on your face?"

"Because, now these days, it is rare to be a virgin when you are in high school and college...and when I tell people I'm still a virgin, they are surprised and asked. 'Really?'" I looked at Nate at the last word, he simply grinned--which took my breath away. Why did he have this effect on me?

"Okay, moving on." He said, helping me climb onto a huge rock. "Any boyfriends?" I stopped short, he glanced nervously at me.

"No boys ever took an interest in me," I said and he started coughing. I laughed at him. "You were eight, Nate."

"Seriously though, you are awesome." He acknowledged to me.

"I don't think guys are simply looking for 'awesome' in girls."

"Let me tell you all the reasons why I think it's mad that guys have never made a move on you." He paused. I nodded at him. "You are really smart, trilingual for now, you speak French, Haitian Creole, English. The fact that you don't wear makeup and you're still so goddamned beautiful is dangerously breathtaking." I smiled at him.

"So, how many girlfriends have you had?" I asked him.

"Three." He simply said.

"Names?" I urged on.

"Well, let's see. My first girlfriend was you, then Lena, and Tessa." I stopped and eyed him.

"Me? What. We were hanging out, having playdates."

"You thought we were having playdates, I counted them as dates."

"We were just friends."

"For you, not for me," he said and I gasped.

"Unbelievable."

"Last time I checked, friends don't have wet kisses, unless they are friends with benefits...is that what we were?" He asked.

"No!" I half-yelled. "Wet kisses?"

"You said it, not me, and I quote 'Fine, it was kind of wet.'"

"So you were eavesdropping," I said. He looked at me in disbelief.

"Of course, I can't help it, I'm half-Vampire."

"Whatever, the kiss was just a bet."

"Yeah, one that had plenty of loopholes to crawl around it." Loopholes? I eyed him carefully. He looked back at me. "Yeah, you could have kissed me on the cheeks, forehead, palm. But instead, you went for my delicious lips." He smirked at me. I looked at him in disbelief.

"I was eight." I said, defending myself.

"Yeah, that didn't stop you." I punched him playfully in his forearm and walked off. "I would not go there if I were you." He warned. I turned and faced him. I was walking backwards.

"Who's going to stop me?" He stared at me. I continued walking backwards. "Nothing can stop me."

"Are you sure about that?" I gave him a careless look. "Come here." He said urgently. He kept glancing at my feet. I looked at my feet and snakes were on the ground...Coral snakes. I screamed.

I ran as fast as I could through the woods, Nate was calling my name, trying to keep up with me. I saw the road ahead, I wanted to get out of the woods. A car was driving, almost hit me, but I jumped so high and managed to do a front flip, and stood on my feet.

I gasped.

The driver was my dad, he had this shock expression on his face. "Hi, dad." I greeted him.

"Hey, Rose. What were you doing?"

"Running from snakes." I said. He nodded, a smile formed on his face.

"I have to talk to your mom." He said as Nate finally reached me.

"You're developing." Nate said when my dad disappeared inside. "You're fast, faster than me."

"Okay, you're only half-Vampire." I said.

"It doesn't matter if I'm half, I still have the same strength and speed as a full one.

"I'm part Werewolf."

"Exactly, you're developing. You're still seventeen, it's not too late to shape-shift."

"Are you saying that I'll be a Wolf-Shifter in no time."

"Yeah and our instincts to hate each other will finally kick in," He said in a serious tone.

"No, it won't. We should have hated each other already." I said. He looked at me. "You're a Protector/Vampire and I am a Minder/Wolf-Shifter."

"And if we still don't hate each other, we're good."

CHAPTER FIVE

School ended, I was waiting for Tia in the parking lot when Tessa came toward me. I pretended that I didn't see her. She stopped in front of me. "Rosabelle," she greeted me.

"Tessa." I looked at her. "What do you want?"

"Nate."

"What can I do about it?"

"Leave him alone."

"I can't do that, he's my best friend--" I told her and she scoffed at me.

"I don't care," She hissed at me. "Stop hanging out with my boyfriend."

"He's not your boyfriend."

"We'll see about that," she said. I saw Tia driving toward us.

I walked away and met Tia half-way. "Are you ready?" She asked.

"I can't wait to start," I smiled at her. She drove. We went to a vast forest, I was a bit uneasy because I was afraid of snakes. "Are there any snakes here."

"This is a forest--" Tia looked at me in disbelief "--of course there are." Tia and I went inside the forest, I looked around nervously, afraid of a snake jumping at me. "Relax, I'll sniff one out before it attacks you." Tia was mocking me.

"This is not funny."

"You're right, it's embarrassing."

"Lots of people are scared of snake," I confirmed.

"Wolf-Shifters aren't supposed to be afraid of them."

"I'm not one yet."

"That's why we are here." Tia said. We walked deeper into the forest, it got darker, I could barely see anything, I had to squint my eyes. "We're having our first lesson--vision." I looked at her with confusion.

"You want me to see the future?"

"Not that kind of vision, I want you to see what's ahead of you." I looked ahead of me, I could not see anything. It was too dark.

"It's dark here, I can barely see anything."

"You are developing, you don't need light to see in the dark, you just need to focus." She instructed me. I took a deep breath and focused on my task. The forest was still dark, but slowly it brightened, it sort of glowed. I gasped. Tia was laughing. "Try to see what's far away."

"I can't do that."

"You are able to see miles ahead of you. Focus." Again, I focused on what was ahead. My vision was blurry, but it slowly became clear. I could see animals, I gasped when I saw a Wolf, he was beautiful. I looked away when he attacked his prey.

"It worked."

"That was today's lesson. You need to practice your vision," Tia told me.

We walked back to the car, we drove in silence to my house. Nate was waiting for me on his front porch, I caught Tia rolling her eyes. "What does that bloodsucker wants?" She murmured under her breath.

"Blood--" Nate said, loud and clear. Tia gasped in total disgust, I was trying to contain my smile.

"Thank you for the day, Tia." I thanked her and quickly got out of the car.

"Bye, Wolf." Nate waved at her.

"Bloodsucker." She spat at him and drove away.

"She hates me, doesn't she?" He asked me.

"No, Nate. She loves you." I sarcastically said.

"Oh, Rosabelle. You and your sarcasm," he said and walked away. I followed him inside his house. "How was your day?"

"I worked on my vision."

"Ah, you can now see in the dark." He said.

How did he know about that? "How do you know about that?" I asked him and he scoffed. He had this arrogant look on his face.

"I'm part Vampire, I have to know these things." He told me, looking at me with uncertainty.

I didn't know much about Vampires, I never really took an interest because I had not shifted yet. "I don't know that much about Vampires," I told him. "Can Vampires be out in the sun?"

"Only eight times a year, the first and the last day of each season--" Nate told me.

"Are they all bad?"

"Yes, they have no morals."

"You don't know that."

"Yes, I do." We went upstairs to his bedroom. "They are all ruthless...just like my biological father." We sat next to each other on the window sill.

"Have you ever met your father?" I asked nervously. I did not know how he was going to react."

"I never met the asshole--" He said, looking away. He was really angry. "And if I did, I would have killed him."

"Don't say that, he's your father."

"He's a rapist," he spat in disgust. "I am the fruit of a rapist." He said in a quiet tone. I didn't know what to say. "Sometimes, I wonder if I disgust my mom. Every time she looks at me...is she remembering the night he raped her?"

"She loves you, Nate. You are the best thing that happened to her in a terrible circumstance." I took hold of his hands. Electricity sparked through my veins and arteries. He looked down at our hands that were intertwined together. He gently squeezed my hands.

"How do you know?"

"She looks at you with admiration, adoration, love." I said. "She could have gotten an abortion or give you up."

"Protectors aren't allowed to do that."

"She's your mother and she loves you." I left him no room to argue with me.

He got up, letting go of my hands. "I know." He walked around the room and pulled out a board game. "It's been years since we've played together."

"Is that Backgammon?" I asked excitedly.

"You know it." He grinned. We sat on the bed, he placed the Backgammon between us. "Do you remember the last time we played this games?"

We had our first kiss on that day, my dad found out about us, that we were friends. It really pissed him off that he decided to have us move to Oregon. "How can I forget?" I asked. "We had our first kiss, my dad caught us and yelled at you, the neighbors called the police, and I had to move."

"We're back at being neighbors again." He smiled. "Roll."

"I don't roll first." I reminded him.

"Right." He rolled and got 16. I rolled and got 64. "Looks like you're going first."

"A good start for me."

~~~

"Bye, bye. Nate is here." I called to my parents.

"Wait." My dad stopped me midway of opening the front door. I turned and faced him. He looked concerned. "You are spending a lot of time with Nate."

"He's my best friend, that's what best friends do." I explained to him.

My dad questioned, "just friends?" I also questioned myself, my body always reacted in a way when I was with Nate, but he never showed me an interest. Yeah, I was certain that we were just friends. "I just don't want you to get hurt."

"He's never going to hurt me."

"You don't know that. He's a Vampire."

"Half," I corrected my dad.

"It doesn't matter, his instincts will be to hurt and kill people." My dad said. He was wrong.

"That's not who Nate is.

"Yet, but he will become one."

"Jesus Christ, dad. Are you hearing yourself?"

"You do not curse our savior in this house."

"Savior my ass." I mumbled and exited my house. Nate was sitting in the driver's seat, looking straight ahead. I close the door after I got inside. "Did you hear anything?" He nodded his head, "I'm sorry."

He quietly said, "Don't be, I'm used to people thinking of me as a monster." He then started driving us to school.

That was really not fair that he had to deal with that. "You are not a monster," I said. I felt bad for Nate, people were judging him as a monster and they did not even know him. It was not fair, he never asked to have this life. "You are not a monster," I said quietly.

"I will be one day."

"Ignore my dad, okay. He's wrong."

"What if he's not."

"I can see the future, Nate. If you were becoming a monster, I would know." He sighed in relief. "It's all about self-control."

We arrived in school. Tessa was waiting for us with her friends. She had her hands on her hips. So dramatic. "Can she be anymore dramatic?" I questioned.

"She actually can." Nate affirmed. We stepped out of the car and made our way inside the school.

"Nate, wait!" Tessa called.

"I can't." Nate said, not looking at her.

"Nate, I'm sorry for what I did." She apologized. Nate turned around and faced her.

"I'm not the one you should apologize to," Nate said. Tessa glanced at me, then back at Nate.

"You can't be serious. I am not going to apologize to that disgusting thing." She said with bitter.

"You better watch your mouth." Nate warned. He was angry, some kids stopped what they were doing. Tessa looked around nervously. "This is the last time that I will hear you say bad words about Belle."

"Belle?" Tessa questioned. "You already have a nickname for her, you just met her weeks ago."

"We met when we were seven years old." Nate corrected her. Tessa had a look of disbelief on her face...and she glared at me.

"She's the girl in the picture that's on your desk in your bedroom," Tessa realized. "You had your first kiss with her...and you expect me to be okay with you hanging out with her?" She asked Nate.

"I don't expect anything from you."

"I won't permit it."

"I'm not asking you for your permission," Nate said.

"I'm forbidding you."

"Pss. You can't tell me what to do."

"I am your girlfriend."

"Ex," Nate corrected. "I broke up with you."

"I thought you said you broke up with him," One of Tessa's friends said and earned a glare from her.

"Mind your fucking business." Tessa warned her. Everyone let out a small gasp. Tessa looked back at Nate. "Nate__"

"Tessa--" Nate interrupted her "--I've moved on."

"Since when?" Tessa half-yelled. She was outraged.

"Since I found out that you slept with your own cousin." There was a mix of reaction in the air. "That is so disgusting, does your parents even know? How can you stay in the same room with him, knowing that his hands were on you, his lips were kissing you, he was moving inside you?"

"Stop it," Tessa demanded. I caught sight of Samantha and Dylan, they were trying hard to contain their laughter.

"And you dare call Belle 'disgusting?'" Nate asked with a total disbelief. He looked straight into Tessa's eyes. "You're the one who's disgusting." Tessa raised her hand up in the air and was mid-way of slapping Nate, but he caught hold of her hand. Everyone gasped. "Don't you even dare," He warned in a low voice. Tessa's eyes widened, Nate let go of her hand and walked away. We all stayed silent and rooted in our spot for seconds.

Tessa approached me, I eyed her. I had no doubt of what she could do to me. "This is all on you." She said icily. Cold chills went through me, but I showed her nothing.

This was not on me, she needed to take responsibility for her own actions and not put blame on someone else. "I never told you to deflower yourself to your cousin." I said and she gasped. I flipped my ponytail__well, my bun at her and walked away with a smile of satisfaction on my face. The bell rang, I went to my first period class. Nate was already sitting down. I sat on my seat. "That was a great performance you did out there." I said and he glared at me.

"Don't start." He warned.

"You should know that I don't do well with warnings." Nate let out a heavy sigh and looked at me__

"You should know that I don't do well with stubbornness." He said.

"Careful or you might become the monster my dad thinks you are," I joked lightly.

"Don't joke about that." He said in a serious tone and I quickly apologized.

"I love drama. Don't you, Nate." Samantha took her seat. Nate rolled his eyes. "Yes, I can be very annoying. I can't argue with that." Samantha was reading his thoughts, Nate glared at her.

"Get out of my mind."

"Why, are there things that you don't want me to know?" Samantha mocked him. "Perhaps__"

"I would think very carefully with your choices of words if I were you." Nate warned. Samantha quickly shut her mouth.

"What's going on?" I asked. Samantha shrugged her shoulders. "Tell me," I insisted.

"I can't, he's blocking me."

"How?"

"He's thinking about a lot of different things," Samantha said. I looked at Nate, he was staring ahead with no expression on his face. He was so beautiful. "Em, em."

"Get out of my head, Samantha."

"If only I could."

The day passed fast, we were all eating lunch. I looked around for any signs of Nate, he was nowhere to be seen. Tessa caught my eyes and glared at me. If looks could kill. "Have any of you seen Nate?" I asked Samantha and Dylan.

"I saw him in the library." Samantha responded.

"Thank you." I got up and left. I could feel someone following me, I turned around and saw Tessa. I rolled my eyes with annoyance, what did she want? Could not she just leave me alone?

"Where are you going?" She asked. I scoffed at her.

"Excuse you?"

"Where are you going?" She asked again.

"I don't have to answer to you," I slowly said.

"I hope you're not going to see Nate." She said. I looked around, the hallway was deserted.

"I am."

"Don't."

"You can't tell me what to do."

"This is my final warning--" she warned me "--stay away from my man."

"He's not yours anymore."

"He's mine, he'll always be mine--" She said in a menacing tone and approached me "--if it wasn't for people around us this morning, I would have made you suffer. Now, stay away from Nate."

"He's moved on from you, don't you get it?"

"Does it look like I care?"

I was so sick of her at this point and wanted to hurt her. "Why don't you go home to your cousin, I'm sure he'll make you feel better--" I spat at her. It was wrong to say that, but she deserved it.

SQUAK

She slapped me and anger rose through me. I felt a form of rage that I've never felt before. In an instant, I attacked her. She fought well, but I was faster and better. "Ahh," I groaned in pain. My brain was on fire, I was hurting really bad. "How do you like that?" Tessa laughed. I felt a small pain in my nails. I looked at them, they were long, curvy, and black. Without thinking, I scratched her arms. My teeth were hurting really bad, I wanted to die. Tessa kicked me in the ribs, I was not hurt, but I was angrier.

I grabbed her by the color of her shirt and bit her neck. She screamed in agony. "Belle, stop." It was Nate. He took hold of me and I pushed him. He flew several feet and hit the ground. He gasped, there was a mix of shock and awe on his face. I could not help but growl at him, my canines were exposed. Tessa looked at me.

"Why is my power not working?" She asked.

"The venom is in you. It's stopping your specialty." Nate took my scarf and put it around Tessa's neck. "Go to the nurse, she'll cure you." Right after Tessa left, an ordinary appeared. Nate quickly pulled me against his chest, I curled my fingers against my palms and my long nails dug through my flesh. "You need to relax and breathe--" Nate said.

I followed his instructions. Slowly, my nails and my teeth went back to normal. "I'm okay now," I said and he let go of me. He observed me for one moment.

"What is wrong with you?"

"Huh?"

"What is wrong with you?" He repeated.

"I'm transforming--" I told him "--I could not control my anger."

"You need to control your anger or you will hurt somebody and I might not be here to stop you."

"I don't need you to be stopped," I said--a bit angry.

"Are you sure?"

"I have to get to class," I said and walked away.

The day passed fast, it was already time to go home. Nate was driving me home, when we arrived, we saw my car in the driveway. "Your car is back." Nate said. I was not expecting it until next week. "I guess I won't be driving you anymore." Nate said. We both got out of the car.

"I guess so." I said. We both said our farewells and walked inside our houses. My mom walked toward me with a smile on her face.

"Did you see your car?"

"It's parked in the driveway, of course, I saw it." I rolled my eyes at her.

"I'm going to pretend that you did not just roll your eyes at me," My mom said.

"I wasn't expecting my car to be ready."

"Your dad brought it."

"Did he?" I asked, smiling a fake smile. My mom knew that smile well.

"Rosie, your dad__"

"Is wrong, don't defend him." I said. "He doesn't like the idea of Nate and I hanging out."

"Can you blame him, he's a Wolf-Shifter. It's in his nature to not like and trust Nate." My mom explained. "He can't help himself."

"That's him, not me." I said. "He has no right to try and ruin my friendship with Nate, he did that once already." The door opened and my dad walked in. "I have homework," I said and headed to my bedroom. I grabbed my art equipment, paints, brushes, and started painting. I grew calmer and less angry. When I was done painting, I let it dry for about fifteen minutes before I hung it up on the wall.

I did my homework and studied for about two hours, my mom came into my room and told me dinner was ready. My mom and my dad chatted throughout dinner, I stayed silent, watching them enjoying each other. "How was your day, Rose?" My dad asked. Before I had a chance to respond, the doorbell rang.

"I hate it when people think they can just interrupt my dinner--" my mom said, getting up. "May I help you?"

"Are you Rosabelle's mother?" A female voice asked.

"Yes."

"We're Tessa's parents." My whole body froze.

"Isn't Tessa the girl who wrecked your car?" My dad asked and I nodded. "I have to see what they have to say." My dad rose, I followed him.

"Come in." My mom invited them in. We all went to the living room. "What brought you two here?"

"Your daughter," Tessa's mom responded.

"What about my daughter?"

"We just wanted to make ourselves clear, if she ever hurts our daughter again, there will be consequences." Tessa's dad warned icily. Chills went down my spine.

"Are you threatening my daughter?" My dad growled, his canines were out. Tessa's parents' eyes widened. "I don't respond well with threats." My mom was smiling proudly.

"I think you're misunderstood, your daughter was the one who hurt my daughter--" my mom started, "--your daughter used her specialty on my daughter and wrecked her car."

"We're talking about what happened today." The dad informed us. Both my mom and dad looked at me with curiosity and back at them. "Your daughter scratched and bit my daughter with her canines."

"What?" Both my mom and dad yelled.

"I only scratched her because she used her specialty on me and slapped me." I defended myself.

"Why did you bit her?"

"She kicked me in the ribs."

"Wait, you scratch her and bit her?" My dad asked in disbelief.

"I was so angry, my nails grew and my teeth turned into canines--" I told him.

"So you scratched and bit her."

"Yes."

"I'm so proud of you." My dad hugged me. "Anne, her canines got out."

"She has both of our traits," my mom said.

"Are you people crazy!" The mother screamed. We all stared at her like she was the one crazy.

"Your daughter should not have slapped Rosabelle," my dad said.

"She had a reason," the dad defended Tessa. My parents looked at them with impatience. "Rosabelle told her to go home to our nephew because he'll make her feel better." My parents gasped and looked at me in shock and disbelief.

"We did not raise you this way." My mom scolded me. I ignored them.

"I only said that because your daughter had sex with your nephew." I told them.

"Excuse us," they both said.

My parents gasped and I looked at my parents--"Yeah, she lost her virginity to her cousin. That is so disgusting." My mom looked at them with sympathy.

"You two need to get out of my house," my mom said. Okay, maybe she was not looking at them with sympathy.

We led them outside of our house. Tessa's mom faced my mom, "Your daughter and your husband are monsters," she said in a loud voice. My mom attacked her with water and she flew backwards.

"Martha," The father shouted and ran toward her. "What is wrong you, people?"

"You're all crazy!" Martha screamed.

"No, bitch. You just bring the worst out of us." We all said the same words at the same time. We were a great example to families out there. The last thing I saw before my mom dragged me inside the house, was Nate and all of his family. His mom, cousins, uncles, and aunts staring at us with shock expressions on their faces.

CHAPTER SIX

Today was Saturday, I climbed on a tree outside and opened my drawing journal. I gasped when I saw a drawing of Martha getting dragged in the air by water. How come I never saw this before, why did I always close my drawing journal after I drew something, it did not make any sense. I tried to draw something, but I could not. I jumped off the tree and started heading back to my house. "No, bitch. You just bring the worst out of us." Someone mocked. Edward was laughing. It was Nate who said that.

"Hey, Nate--" I greeted and he walked toward me.

"I really like that part." He smiled.

"It was funny," I admitted. "What are you doing?"

"Nothing."

"Actually, we were going to a party." Edward said.

"What party?"

"Just a local pool party--" Nate said "--wanna come?"

"Sure." I said.

We climbed in Nate's car. Edward and Nate sat on the front, I took the back seat. Nate and Edward talked and joked around, they were ignoring me. I was not complaining. Edward eyed my lap and grabbed my drawing journal. "Hey." I protested.

"Give it back, Edward." Nate said. Edward was not listening. He was going through every single drawings I ever drew.

"Dude, she's a psycho." Edward pointed a finger at me. Nate slapped his finger away and shook his head. "She has like twenty drawings of you."

"So?" Nate asked.

"I think she likes you," he whispered.

"It's not that--" I screamed, panicking. Nate slammed on the brake. He and Edward looked at me. I felt so uncomfortable. Why did I panic in the first place. "I'm a Minder."

His green eyes were mocking me, "And your specialty is drawing?" I wanted nothing more than to yank his dark hair. "That is so embarrassing," he continued to turn pages and then he stopped. "What the heck?" He gasped. Nate snuck a peek and smiled. I looked over Edward's shoulder. It was a drawing of him looking through my drawings. I could not remember me drawing this.

"Belle draws the future," Nate informed him. Edward looked at me in awe.

"Not so embarrassing now, is it?" I mocked. He handed me back my drawing.

"Draw my future wife," he demanded.

"Excuse you?"

"Please," he sighed in annoyance.

"My specialty does not work like that."

"Then it's an embarrassment," I gasped at him. Nate glared at him, but behind his glare, there was humor.

"We're here," Nate announced--parking his car. We got out of the car. "Did you bring a swimsuit?" He asked me, I shook my head--"How are you going to swim?"

"I don't know how to swim, remember?" I reminded him.

"Black people," Edward chuckled. Nate and I ignored him.

"Don't pay attention to him, Belle." Nate said.

"Belle?" Edward questioned. "You still call her that?"

"What's wrong with that?"

"Do you know the meaning of 'Belle' in English?" It means 'beautiful' and she is__" I didn't let him finish the sentence, my hand struck against his cheek and lower jaw.

SQUAK

I slapped him. His face turned left, his hand immediately reached his face and lower jaw. Nate was trying hard not to laugh, he put a hand on my back and guided me away. I looked back at Edward, "Later, Eddie." Edward glared at me and I laughed with satisfaction.

"Don't push him." Nate warned me.

"What is he going to do?"

"I'm not the Seer here."

"Smart," I applauded him.

The pool party was great, I had a lot of fun, I danced around. I pretty much took the dance floor to myself___I was drunk. I was dancing like a mad girl, some people laughed at my dance moves, but I was too drunk to care. Nate was nowhere to be seen, I saw Edward gliding toward me, I glared at him and he raised his hands up.

"Look at her. She and Nate are yelling at each other." He pointed at a girl, I looked over and saw Tessa. She looked pissed and was yelling at Nate. What was going on?

"That's Tessa, his ex." I responded.

"I know who she is, I cannot stand her." He looked unsatisfied. "You know, she is not that good looking."

"Really?"

"Yeah, you're prettier than her and that's saying a lot--" He laughed and I joined in. Tessa caught me watching her. She started advancing me. "I'm out of here."

"You BITCH," Tessa screamed at me. She always had to make a scene.

"Lower your voice, you're making a scene." I said, clutching my ears.

"I don't give a FUCK." She screamed. She had to drop the F-bomb. "You should have kept your mouth shut."

She was the one who told her parents that I told her to go home to her cousin, I had to explain why. "Well, I didn't. What are you going to do about that?" I asked her with defiance. I was on the edge of the pool.

"You asked for it." She said and pushed me into the pool, but I managed to pull her in with me.

Everyone cheered. Nate grabbed my hands and pulled me out. "That was so much fun." I slurred and giggled. Nate wrapped a towel around me.

"You're drunk, I'm taking you home." He led me away from the pool, Edward followed us.

"Don't take me home," I whined.

"Trust me, I don't want to take you home." Nate said.

"Then why are you?"

"Because I don't want your dad to kill me twice," I laughed really loud.

"Twice, is that even possible?"

"You're really drunk, aren't you?" He asked.

"I am," I giggled.

Nate drove me home and helped me inside my house. My dad saw the state I was in and glared at Nate.

"What happened to her?" He demanded.

"She got drunk."

"Why did you let her get drunk?"

"It was not his fault, dad. I had fun today." I defended Nate. My dad looked disappointed in me.

"I'm sure you did." My dad said, a bit angrily. "Go to your room."

"Sir, you don't have to be angry with Belle."

"This is none of your business, Vampire."

"Half."

"I don't care, stay away from my daughter--" my dad warned.

"Dad__"

"Go to your room," I stared blankly at my dad.

"Don't worry, sir. I'm leaving." Nate said and left. I ran after him and called his name. "You're going to be in more trouble if you don't go back inside." He told me.

"I don't care."

"You need to go to bed and sleep. You have a big day tomorrow," he told me.

"Rosabelle, get back in here." My dad called.

I let out a huge sigh. "I have to go." I went back inside. "What's wrong with you?" I asked my dad.

"I don't want you hanging out with him anymore."

"You can't tell me who I can or can't hang out with." I told him in defiance.

"I am your father."

"Start acting like one," I said and ran upstairs to my room. I slammed the door shut and jumped on my bed. My dad was being really unfair.

~~~

On Sunday, I woke up with a massive hangover. The sunlight was too bright for my eyes, I groaned in pain. "Rosabelle, your dad wants you to help him with breakfast." My mom came into my room. I groaned. "How's your headache?" My mom handed me a glass of water. I drank it.

"Terrible."

"Why did you drink?"

"I wanted to have fun."

"Did you?"

"I made a fool of myself," I told her. "I'm going back to sleep, I'm tired."

"Your dad__"

"Can't he make breakfast by himself?" I asked. My mom gave me an exasperated sigh. My dad could not cook anything, we could never trust him with cooking. The last time he cooked breakfast, it was a disaster.

"You know what happens when he tries to cook." My mom reasoned with me.

"Do you even know what he did?" I asked her.

"He told me when I came home from work--" she said "--he wants to apologize."

"He does?" I asked. My mom nodded her head. I got out of bed. "I have to hear that."

My mom and I headed to the kitchen, we found my dad in a state of panic, he was waving a cloth in the air. There was a lot of smoke. "Lucien, what are making to cause all that smoke?" My mom asked.

"Omelet," he responded.

Mom and I looked at each other and rolled our eyes. "That is the easiest thing to cook," my mom told my dad in a disapproving tone.

My dad looked impatient. "Are you seeing all this?" He raised his hands up in the air. My mom and I looked at the smoke that was above our heads. "This is not easy--" he now pointed at the omelet.

"Which is why you need to take cooking class," my mom said.

That was not a good idea, I could not imagine a happy ending with my dad taking cooking class. "Are you serious?" My dad asked. My mom looked around the kitchen and back at him with her eyebrows raised. "Do you want me to burn down the class?"

"I certainly don't want you to burn this whole house down," my mom voiced her wants.

"Mom, I don't think dad going to cooking class is a good idea," I said. "The last thing I want is for us to get sued because dad burned down the building."

"Okay, Rosabelle, can you help your dad with breakfast, I have work to do in my office." My mom left.

My dad and I cleaned up the kitchen, before making pancakes. We worked together in silence, not saying a word to each other. We were putting breakfast on the table when my dad started talking. "I want you to distance yourself from Nate," my dad said. I stared at him with my mouth gaped open.

"I should have known better when my mom said you were going to apologize."

"I am apologizing."

"Really, are you?"

"I just don't want you to get hurt," he sincerely said.

"How many times do I have to tell you that Nate is never going to hurt me, he's not the monster you make him out to be." I defended Nate.

"Physically, but not emotionally." My dad said. I looked at him with confusion. "He might not hurt you physically, but he will hurt you emotionally."

"Why would you say that?"

"When you fully transform, both of your instincts will kick in and you will hate each other. You may not believe me now, but you will, and you'll get hurt."

"Why do you think I'll be hurt?" I asked him.

He looked away for a moment. "Because I see the way you look at him," he whispered. I stared at my dad.

"I look at Nate the same way I look at almost everybody."

"No, you don't. You look at him differently." My dad looked at me. "You look at him with admiration...and your eyes glow a bit."

"My eyes glow?"

"It's a Wolf thing and that's how I know you have feelings for him." I didn't know what to say. "That's why I need you to stay away from him. If you don't want to do it for me, do it for the sake of your heart__" he advised me and left to tell my mom that breakfast was ready.

After breakfast, I went upstairs, brushed my teeth, and took a shower. I went back into my bedroom and saw Nate sitting on his window sill. I walked over to my window. he heard me approaching and looked at me. "Hi, how are you?"

"I'm fine."

"I'm sorry about yesterday."

"It's fine," he said and left, just like that. What was going on with him?

~~~

Today was Monday, I drove myself to school and parked in my usual spot. It probably wasn't a good idea since last time I had parked in this spot, my car had turned into a wreck. But I did not care, I would have an opportunity to ride with Nate again. I went to my locker and thought about my weekend, it was crazy. "I love your mom." Samantha appeared out of nowhere and startled me. "And is it wrong to say that I am happy for what you did to Tessa?"

"It's not wrong."

"Please, don't ever bite me, I won't be able to tolerate the pain--" Samantha told me.

"Don't worry about it," I assured her.

Dylan came toward us with a huge smile on his face. "Let me guess, you met a girl last night--" Samantha said, a little annoyed.

"That was not really guessing, but you know it." Dylan grinned and Samantha rolled her eyes.

"What's her name?" I asked.

"Her name is Laurie. She's a freshman in college," Dyan said proudly.

"She's in college." Samantha gaped.

"I scored really good."

"She's older than you."

"When a girl is dating an older guy in college, it's a proud thing, but when a guy is dating an older girl in college, people make a big deal out of it."

"It's just that your maturity level is different," Samantha told him.

"What about it?"

Samantha was about to hurt his pride, "I'm younger than you and I have more maturity. She is two years older than you, can you imagine the level of maturity she has." Samantha really needed to stop talking. She glared at me, of course, she heard that.

"I am mature."

"For a guy."

"She's only two years older."

"Two more years of wisdom."

"I can't believe you right now," Dylan said and left.

Samantha looked at me, "What did I do?"

I ignored her question, "You like him."

"What, no I don't."

"You're jealous of Laurie."

"We need to go to class." She dragged me to class.

When I entered class, my eyes automatically fell on Nate, he was glaring at me. Samantha whispered to me, "He's pissed." I sat down and greeted him. "Why did you park in Tessa's spot today?" He asked.

"The parking lot is for students."

"I don't have time for your sassiness today," he was glaring at me.

"I don't have time for your interrogation."

"You really don't want to try me," he warned and I did not like that.

"Is that a threat?" I growled at him. He stared at me.

"Control yourself...Wolf," he snarled at me.

The way he said it...He said it with so much disgust and it hurt my feelings. In that moment, I wanted to hurt his feelings. "Bloodsucker," I growled and he glared at me. He looked hurt. Suddenly, he got up and left.

CHAPTER SEVEN

I knocked on his bedroom, my dad was going to kill me if he knew where I was. "Come in," he answered and I walked into his bedroom. He was lying on his back on the bed, he sat up and glared at me. "What are you doing here?"

"I came here to apologize. I should not have called you that." I apologized.

"But, you did."

"And I'm sorry."

"I don't want your apology."

"Nate, don't be like that--" I pleaded.

"Get out," he commanded. I stared at him. Was he for real? I was truly hurt in that moment.

"Are you serious?"

"Dead serious," he said. "Now get out."

"No." I stood my ground. He advanced me, my heart picked up, he looked menacing. I did not know what he was going to do.

"Your heartbeat is really fast, you're afraid of me because just like your dad and pretty much everyone else, you think of me as a monster."

"I don't think of you as a monster."

"Your words are meaningless to me, your body is trembling with fear--" he said "--go before I turn into the monster you think of me."

"Nate__"

"I'm not telling you again," he snarled at me. I ran from his house to mine.

I slammed the front door to my house shut. "Rosabelle, what's wrong?" My mom asked. I ignored her and went to my bedroom. She followed me. From the look I gave her she already figured it was Nate. "What did he do?"

"I called him a bloodsucker and he got really upset, he doesn't want to talk to me." I shook my head slightly. "I went to his house and apologized. He did not want my apology and told me to get out." I told my mom.

"Why would you call him that in the first place?" My mom asked me.

"He called me a 'Wolf.'"

"Maybe he was playing."

"No, mom. You should have seen his face when he called me that...he had this look of disgust written on his face."

My mom stayed quiet for a moment. "You are developing, Rosabelle. This is why your dad is against you hanging out with Nate. Because at the end of the day, you two are going to hate each other."

"I don't want to hate him, I don't want him to hate me." I told her.

"Why?" She asked me. I looked at the window, it was opened and I knew Nate was listening. I grabbed a piece of paper, a pen, and wrote.

I have feelings for him.

I handed my mom the piece of paper and she read it. Her eyes widened. "You do?" She whispered and I nodded. "Your dad is going to be mad."

"He already knows."

"You told him before me." My mom sounded offended.

"No, mom. He knew because of my eyes."

"They glow when you look at him," she whispered. "Why are you risking your heart?"

"I can't help myself, my heart wants him--" I whispered quietly to her. The doorbell rang, my mom and I went downstairs. I opened the door. It was Tia picking me for further lesson.

We walked through the forest and stopped several minutes later. "Have you been practicing your vision?" I told her 'yes.' "Good. Today, we'll be working on your smell. As Wolf-Shifters, we depend on our noses. We use our noses as a tracking method."

"Okay."

"Tell me what you smell." I was now focused. I breathed in the environment.

"I smell trees."

"Anyone can smell trees, this is a forest after all. What do you smell?"

I took a deep breath, "I smell something wet, like a dog." I crinkled my nose. Something caught my nose and my mouth watered. "Someone's cooking spaghetti."

"Tell me where," Tia demanded. I took a deep breath, it took me several seconds to know.

"Nate."

"I'm assuming he's your Vampire friend," Tia assumed.

"We're not friends anymore."

"It's for the best."

"Is it?" I asked.

~~~

I parked my car in the usual spot, Dylan and Samantha met me at my car. We greeted each other. Today was a really cold day and I liked it. Samantha and Dylan were shivering. "Aren't you cold?" Samantha asked.

"She's a Wolf-Shifter." Dylan said as if that would explain everything.

"What's going on with you two?" I asked.

"I'm failing Organic Chemistry," Samantha announced.

"I told you not to take that class," Dylan said.

"You know I don't always listen to you."

"You need to start."

"You two will make a cute couple," I said for the sake of Samantha.

She glared at me, I glared back and she knew what I was doing. "Samantha and I could never happen--" Dylan said. Samantha stared at him. I did not know how she was feeling, she was hiding her emotions. "I'm not matured enough for her," Dylan said and I laughed. Samantha had it coming. I saw Nate's car coming our way. He parked next to my car and got out. He gave me his signature glare and walked away.

Samantha and Dylan looked at me with confusion. "He's being like this with me since my dad told him to stay away from me," I told them.

"Can't you read his mind?" Dylan asked Samantha.

"He's been blocking me," Samantha responded.

In class, Nate ignored me, he pretended that I did not exist. I was getting really pissed now, how dared he ignore me. Samantha kept me company. Nate was sitting between us, but we managed to talk, he was reading a book. "Can you both sit down properly and be quiet. I am trying to read a book." Nate said with frustration. He was pissed all the time and I had enough.

"When was the last time you had sex because you're annoyed all the time." I asked. Samantha chuckled and he glared at me.

"This is none of your business."

"It is when you're making me your victim," I told him. I was not going to back down.

"Oh, I'm sorry. Does princess Rosabelle wants to be treated like a queen?" He mocked.

"Seriously, what's going on with you?"

"It's none of your business."

"Just tell me," I urged him.

That was not a good idea because he gave me a cold look. "This is my problem with you, you never know when to mind your own damn business." He was being cold with me and I needed to take a hint.

"I could say the same thing about you," I scoffed at him. What was wrong with him. "Is this about what my dad said...because I don't care."

"You wanna know what's wrong with me?" He asked and I nodded. "You...you are what's wrong with me?" He said as the bell rang and left. I stared after him.

"He can't stand me." I whispered to Samantha--who then told me I needed to ignore him. "Why is he being this way?"

"He's part Vampire and you're transforming into a Werewolf, Shape-Shifter, Wolf-Shifter...whatever you call yourselves these days." Samantha started.

"All of the above, but we prefer the term Shape-Shifter or Wolf-Shifter." I confirmed.

We started walking to our next class. "His instincts are kicking in and yours will too." Samantha told me. It was probably true, but I did not want that.

"I'm not ready for that," I said. "He has been a bit aggressive lately."

"Vampires are supposed to be monsters, killing ordinaries, etcetera." Samantha shrugged her shoulders.

"He's part Protector, Protectors protect ordinaries from demons and Supernaturals like us--" I defended Nate.

I was sick of people thinking of him as a monster. "I know you have feelings for him and you don't want to look past the truth, but you two have different fates, and your fates don't belong in the same world--" Samantha said and walked into her class.

~~~

I was walking to my car when Tessa approached me. "I hear there's trouble in paradise."

I really hated that saying. Tessa needed to stop being so over-the-top when it came with Nate. He and I were never dating to begin with. "Nate and I were never dating." I told her.

"Good, keep it that way." She said and walked away. I saw Nate walking to his car, he was still ignoring me. We both got into our cars and drove home.

Nate was about to get inside his house__"Nate, can we talk." I approached his front door, he got inside and closed the door on my face. I knocked on the door repeatedly, but no one would answer. I stopped knocking, went to the corner of his house where his bedroom window was. I thanked God there was a tree as I used it to climb to his bedroom.

The window was opened. When I snuck a look inside his bedroom, I saw him standing in front of me with his arms crossed over his chest. I yelped. "You have no limits, do you?" He asked.

I fully entered his bedroom, "I want to talk to you."

"I don't want to talk."

"You can fight your instincts," I urged.

"I don't want to."

"Do it for me." I advanced him.

"Why would I do anything for you?" He asked. His eyes were so beautiful. I advanced him further. "Why are you advancing me?" \ don't know, I shrugged my shoulders at him.

My feet were moving on their own, I just could not control them. "Your eyes are glowing." He looked at me in wonder and I smiled.

"I know." We were really close now.

"Why are they glowing?"

"Because of this," I kissed him on the lips.

He place his hands on my waist. A moment later, I was flown backwards and broke his bedroom door. Shock went through my body, I slowly got up. "Get out," he whispered. I looked at him with a shock expression on his face.

"What."

"You heard me."

"I just kissed you."

"I never told you to."

"I have feelings for you."

"I don't care," he said. It was like he stabbed me. "Go, don't make me repeat myself," he warned. I looked at him, he had no expression on his face and in that moment, I realized that my dad and Samantha were right, I was letting my feelings for him blind me from the truth. He truly was a monster.

"I won't." I whispered and left.

~~~

Yesterday, after my humiliation, I had gone home and cried. I just could not believe that Nate reacted this way, he now knew my feelings for him. I decided to walk to school today, I needed to take my mind off things. I had my headphones on, listening to NF. He was my favorite rapper.

I still had my headphones on when I opened my locker, I grabbed what I needed and put away what I didn't need. I went to my first class. Nate never showed up. He ditched first period and I knew it was because of me.

I didn't talk to anyone so far, not even Samantha. I was too angry, sad, and heartbroken.

At lunch, Dylan, Samantha and I sat at our regular table. I was having peanut butter and jelly sandwich and I was not enjoying it. "Rosabelle, are you okay?" Dylan asked. He was observing me.

"No, she's heartbroken." Samantha answered for me. "Yesterday, after he told her that she was the problem, she went to his house and he shut the door on her face. She climbed up to his bedroom window__"

"Stop right there--" Dylan said and looked at me. "Have you no shame?" He asked me. "When a guy tells you that you're a problem and shut his front door in your face, that's a sign that you need to stay away from him."

"That's what I told her," Samantha said.

"No, you did not." I earned a glare from her. She looked at Dylan with a smile on her face.

"You have to hear the best part."

"Samantha, shut up."

"After she climbed up to his bedroom, she kissed him and he pushed her away." Dylan gasped. "When he pushed her away with his Vampire strength, she broke the door with her Werewolf strength--" Samantha told him and I rolled my eyes.

"You need to stop reading my mind," I told her.

"I can't. Drama's always following you."

"She loves drama--" Dylan said, rolling his eyes.

"How's everything with Laurie?" I asked Dylan. Samantha scoffed and rolled her eyes. Dylan showed me a picture of a girl on his phone. "She's hot." I said and earned a glare from Samantha.

"Tell me about it." He showed me another picture of a guy. He was not good looking.

"Who is that?" Samantha asked.

"The guy she finds attractive," Dylan said those words in a way that made me and Samantha laughed.

"Is she blind?" Samantha asked.

"Look at me," Dylan commanded. We looked at him. "I'm really attractive." Samantha nodded her head in agreement. I rolled my eyes. "Why did you roll your eyes?" Dylan asked me.

"She has feelings for Nate, the hottest guy in school. She was comparing you with him."

"No, I was not."

"Last time I checked, I'm the one who can read minds here." Samantha reminded me.

"Not everyone finds someone attractive by their looks on the outside--" I said and they both scoffed at me.

"Says the girl who has feelings for Nate," Dylan said.

"Look where that got me," I murmured.

"You and me both." Dylan said. He was thinking about Laurie. Samantha had a smile on her face. Dylan and I stared at her. "Why are you smiling?"

"Oh, me. I just believe that it's for the better." Samantha told him. "Just yesterday you were talking over and over about her and now you are a loner." She laughed and Dylan glared at her. "You're like Rosabelle." I gasped.

"I am not a loner." I defended myself.

"Whatever, the people you like have interests in others," She said and nodded her head to a direction. I looked over and saw Nate, flirting with Tessa. My heart boiled with anger. How could he? I had just kissed him yesterday. "It was just yesterday that you kissed him and now he's flirting with his ex." Samantha said.

"I have to go to the library." I got up and started leaving. When I looked back, Nate was still flirting with Tessa.

I walked home after school, I was halfway to my house when Nate drove by. He stopped the car. "Hey, do you want a ride?" He asked. I looked at him in disbelief. It was just yesterday that he had thrown me across his room and told me to get out...and now__

"Are you serious?"

"I would not ask if I wasn't."

"No thanks."

"It's a long way to walk."

"I'll be fine," I told him and continued walking.

"Belle__"

"Don't you dare call me that," I spat at him. "I told you about my feeling for you, I kissed you, you pushed me and told me to get out, and today you were flirting with Tessa."

"I can flirt with whoever I want."

"Leave me alone, Nate, the last thing I want is to sit next to you in a car--" I told him.

"Fine," I heard him said with bitter and drove away.

When I got home, I went to my mom's study room and did my home works. After that, I decided to cook dinner. I was cooking my favorite food, spaghetti. I was halfway done when my parents showed up, my mom decided to help me. I was not complaining. My dad was standing in the kitchen, watching us attentively. "Can I help?" He asked. My mom and I looked at him. Was he serious? Indeed he was.

"No," My mom and I said in unison. We could not afford any catastrophe.

"Okay," my dad retreated.

We ate dinner as a family, we talked to each other, dinner was really fun. My mom asked me about school and I told her it went fine. "You left your car here, did you get a ride?" My dad asked. I knew he was thinking about Nate.

"No, I felt like walking."

"Tia told me that you and Nate are no longer friends," he said. My mom stared at me.

"What happened?" She asked.

"His instincts are kicking in," I told them.

"It's only a matter of time before your instincts kick in," my dad said.

"He ditched first period because I was going to be in the class."

"That's normal."

"I just don't understand how this can happen." I really could not understand.

"He's part Vampire."

"Now you're calling him 'part Vampire,'" I scoffed in disbelief.

"And you're developing into a Wolf-Shifter." He ignored what I had just said.

"Three days ago, we were hanging out together, having fun, enjoying each other's company, and now he hates me and can't stand me."

"That's how it usually works."

"It's really confusing."

"It won't be for long." My dad assured me.

"Will we hate each other forever?" I asked. I was holding my breath, I didn't want to breathe.

"Yes."

"Can we control our instincts?"

"Even if we can, we don't want to." What did he mean by that, "Because we love hating each other." He responded.

CHAPTER EIGHT

"Can you hear anything specific?" Tia asked. We were at the mall, working on my hearing. The mall was packed with people and I could not hear anything specific. All I heard was the sound of muffles and laughter.

"I hear laughter." I responded.

"Do you hear anything else?"

"No."

"Focus on one conversation," I navigated my way through conversations.

"Nate, you're funny--" I heard someone said. I recognized that voice, I used my vision and searched the crowd. I saw them standing in front of Victoria Secret. I could never picture Nate going there.

"I'm actually not."

"I'm happy that you forgave me for what I did," she smiled at him.

"Everyone makes mistake."

"I'm really glad we're back together," She said and I gasped. Nate looked around as if he had heard me gasp, but he had not seen me.

"Me too." He did not just say that, how could he say that after everything she did, she slept with her cousin for God's sake.

"I can't wait to see the look on Rosabelle's face when she learns about us," Tessa said.

"I think she already knows," Nate was now looking at me. My heart was beating fast, Tessa had a victory smirk on her face. I rolled my eyes and walked away, Tia followed me.

"She's a Minder, Isn't she?" Tia asked, I simply nodded. "What's her specialty?"

"She can make you feel like your brain is on fire." I told her. She looked surprised. Tessa had a really nice specialty.

"She doesn't like you, right?"

"Nope."

"Has she ever used her specialty on you?"

"Twice."

"Did it hurt?"

"My brain was like on fire, of course, it did." I told her, reliving the memories.

"What did you do?"

"The first time, I did nothing, but the second time, I bit her." I told Nina and she laughed.

"I would have done the same thing," she told me and I joined her laughter.

"I stopped her specialty," I told her.

"That's one of the perks of being what we are, if we bite a Minder, their specialty won't be responding for a week--" she told me.

"Are you serious?" She nodded her head and gave me a mischievous smile. I could not believe it. "That is so cool." I had one victim in my head. "I can bite Tessa every week then."

"The one who can burn brains?"

"Who else?" I smiled.

~~~

"Hey, Rosabelle--" Samantha greeted me, we were having lunch. She sat down next to me and I greeted her back. "Guess who's back together," Samantha told me to guess. I already knew the answer.

"Who?"

"You have to guess."

"Just tell me."

"Nate and Tessa are back together," She announced.

Dylan had a disgusted look on his face. "If I were him, I would have never gotten back with her--" he said.

"You're definitely not him," Samantha said. "Unlike Nate, you have morality."

"I'm sitting right here," I reminded them. I didn't want to hear them talking bad about Nate. I had feelings for him after all.

"She does not want us talking about Nate." Samantha told Dylan.

"Us? You were the one talking lowly of him," Dylan told Samantha. I smiled.

"Why are you smiling?" Samantha asked me.

"Nothing," I replied.

I noticed Tessa walking in the cafeteria, a girl accidentally dumped her tray on her, the whole cafeteria went silent. "You little__"

BEEP

The bell rang and the girl quickly rushed out of the cafeteria. Tessa walked away with a scowl on her face. We all walked back to class.

~~~

I was in the forest, running with all I had. I was fast, I loved the feeling of my feet hitting the ground. I was barefoot, the ground felt really good, I enjoyed it. I sprinted faster than ever. Trees rushed past me, the wind was hitting me. I was blindsided with joy that I did not see someone running. A moment later, I collided with someone, whoever that was, knocked my breath away and there was a lot of pain throughout my body. I laid on the ground, gasping for air. "Belle, I didn't see you on time." I recognized that voice. I looked up and saw Nate.

"I didn't see you on time either," I managed to say. He helped me on my feet. "Thank you." I thanked him.

"You're welcome." He said. I looked him deep in the eyes. He was still holding my hands from helping me up. "Are you okay?"

"I'm in a lot of pain right now."

"We were both going fast." He said. "I'm stronger than you, you're faster than me."

"Speed and strength are not a good combination after all," I told him.

"I never thought it was." He looked at me. All I felt was spark and electricity flowing through my body. How was that even possible?

"I have to go." I said and limped away.

"Let me help you."

"No, I'm fine."

"You can barely walk."

"One of the reasons why I'm limping."

"Let me carry you," he offered.

I stopped limping. Nate, carrying me, my arms around him, there was nothing I wanted more than that. I stared at him for a moment. "I don't think that's appropriate." I told him.

"Why not?"

"Don't you have a girlfriend or something?" I asked and limped back to my house, leaving him staring after me.

~~~

Two days later, Tia and I were in the forest, we were preparing to race each other. I knew I could beat her, I was fast. "Ready?" Tia asked and I nodded. "Go." We ran as fast as we could, she was ahead of me, maybe I underestimated her. About four seconds later, I surpassed her. I could tell she was surprised. I saw my house in the distance and ran toward it.

I stopped dead on my tracks, my heart was breaking at the sight in front of me. Tia halted in her tracks when she saw me watching Nate and Tessa, kissing. No, they were not kissing, they were shoving their tongues into each other's throat. As if he was aware of my presence. He looked straight at me. "I hope you're happy." I muttered and disappeared into the forest.

CHAPTER NINE

I walked back in the forest, Tia was following me. I heard her take a deep breath. "You have feelings for him," she stated. I stopped walking and stared at her. "Don't deny it, I saw your eyes."

"I wasn't denying anything."

"You weren't admitting anything either."

"I didn't have to," I shut her up.

"Why would you risk your heart like that?"

"Excuse me?"

"Why would you risk it?"

"I can't help myself, my heart wants him and no one else. I never planned to have feelings for him--" I told Tia and she scoffed at me.

"Yeah, but you could have prevented it."

I stared at her in disbelief. "Have you ever heard of the saying 'you can't help who you fall for.' The heart wants what it wants, and right now, my heart wants him. How could I have prevented it?"

"You're part Wolf-Shifter and a Minder, he's part Vampire and Protector, you are natural enemies both ways."

"I know, but Tessa is a Minder."

"He's half Protector," she reminded me. "I think he's more of a Vampire than a Protector...he was kissing a Minder and he can't stand you," She told me and it was the truth. Maybe. We stayed silent for a minute, gazing at each other. "What is it about him? What made you have feelings for him?"

"He's part Protector and Protectors protect ordinaries from Supernaturals." I told her half the truth. She gave me an impatient look. "We met when we were seven years old, we were best friends for a year, and he was my first kiss."

"I know the story. Your dad caught you two kissing and he decided to move to Oregon." It was the truth, there was something that I needed to ask her.

"Why is everyone telling me that I'm risking my heart by having feelings for him?" I asked Tia.

"It's simple. When you are a Wolf-Shifter, your emotions are heightened. When you hate, you really hate, and you're going to hate. But when you love, you really love. Right now, you have feelings for him and the more you are transforming, the more your feelings will grow, and you might fall in love with him if you have not already. I mean, your eyes are already glowing when you look at him."

"What happens after that?"

"When you transform, you will really hate him and really love him at the same time."

"A love/hate relationship."

"Worse," Tia muttered. "Your mind will think of him as the enemy, it'll make you hate him. Your heart will beat for him, it'll make you love him. Your body will follow your instincts and reject his presence, but at the same time, because of your feelings for him, it will crave for his touch." Tia told me. This sounded horrible.

"I will be able to control myself."

"Your heart, body, and mind can't work separately. They all work together. That's what makes us who we are." Tia told me. I thought about everything.

"What will happen to me?"

"You have no idea what it can do to you, you will have a broken heart every day for a long time. Every time you hear him, see him, feel his presence, the more effect it will have on you." She told me.

"What can I do to stop it?" I asked. I wanted to know, I needed to know.

"You still have not transformed yet, so you still have time--" she told me "--you can still move on. Date someone."

"I've never gone on a date before," I told her.

"Your boyfriends never took you on a date before?" She asked and I looked away, embarrassed.

"I've never had a boyfriend."

"Never?" She gasped.

"No."

"There's a first time for everything." She told me.

~~~

"He's your Nate after all, Rosabelle--" Samantha said. We were at my locker, I was ready to go home.

"He's not mine, he's Tessa's--" I told her.

"I'm no one's," A voice said, startling us. It was Nate. "Can we talk?" He asked me.

"No." I told him and he gave me a cold look.

"I want to talk to you."

"And I don't want to talk to you," I told him icily. I didn't want to risk my heart with him.

"I don't care that you don't want to talk to me--" he told me, staring at me straight in the eyes.

"Are we really doing this right now?"

"I don't know, are we?"

"Leave her alone, she doesn't want to talk to you." Samantha cut in. Nate stared at her.

"Mind your business," he spat at her and Samantha cowered herself. I felt bad for her.

"Don't be mean to my friend," I warned. "What do you want to talk about anyway?" I asked him.

"What happened on Monday," he said. "Let's go somewhere to talk."

"I already know what happened between you two." Samantha said.

"Shh." I shushed her.

"I'm not talking in front of her," Nate said and walked away.

I knew I had to follow him, so I did. A moment later, he pulled me inside a closet and switched on the light. I looked at my surroundings. We were inside the janitor's closet. "Oh, wow. The janitor's closet." I looked at Nate and smiled at him. "Are we going to make out?" I asked, still smiling. He stared impassively at me, my smile faltered. "I was just joking," I quickly told him.

"Don't joke about that," he told me.

"Sorry." I apologized. "What did you want to talk about?"

"About Monday."

"What about Monday?" I asked.

"You kissed me." I know. "And I pushed you away...I should not have done that--" he said and I had to agree.

"You told me to get out, and that you did not care about my feelings for you."

"You kissed me," he accused.

"Because I have feelings for you," I told him.

"I never told you to have feelings for me."

I looked at him in disbelief. "Do you think I wanted to have feelings for you?" I asked him. "I didn't choose to have feelings for you."

"And yet you do," he said. You need to move on because I'm not interested in you."

"This is why I hate talking to you, we always get into a fight, and you end up hurting my feelings." I told him. He looked like he cared for a moment.

"That's because you always expect something from me," he said--closing his eyes. "I can't give you what you want, I can't have feelings for you."

"You can't or you don't want to?"

"Both," he answered.

We stayed quiet for a minute, just staring at each other. "You can't tell me you feel nothing for me," I told him. We stood motionless for a moment before he advanced me. I backed away and hit the wall. He was close to me. I looked up at him and saw my eyes through his eyes. They were glowing. A moment later, his lips were on mine. I kissed him with all I had. One of his hands was on my neck, the other one was on my lower back--pulling me closer. I clutched my hands on his triceps.

All I felt was electricity, spark, things that I could not define, I was alive. I placed my hands around his shoulders and kissed him deeper. A moment later, he broke away and looked at me in the eyes. "I feel nothing," he said. I gasped in shock. A moment later, he left. I sank to the floor and started crying. I felt humiliated, how could he do that to me? He should not have kissed me if he was going to do that. After everything that happened between us...I clutched on my stomach so I would not scream.

I felt anger, my canines were free. I wanted nothing more than to rip something apart. I wanted his head.

I cried for about fifteen minutes before I left. I went home, ate a cinnamon poptart, and took a nap. Fifteen minutes later, There was a knock on my door. I let out a groan. The door opened and Tia walked in. "What do you want?" I demanded.

"Good afternoon to you too," she said sarcastically.

"What are you doing here?"

"We have training remember?" She reminded me. I let out a groan, I forgot all about that.

"Sorry, I forgot."

"It's okay, I'll just wait for you." Tia said. The last thing I wanted to do now was more training. All I wanted to do, was stay in bed and sleep.

"Can we do this another time? I don't feel like doing anything today." I told her. She observed me for a minute.

"What's going on, were you crying?"

"I don't want to talk about it," I told her. She came and sat on my bed.

"What happened?"

"Nate."

"Does he know you have feelings for him?"

"Yes."

"How, you told him?"

"And kissed him," I added and she took a deep breath. I looked away for a moment.

"How did he respond?"

"He flew me across his room and I broke his bedroom door." I told Tia and she gasped. "He told me to get out and that he didn't care about my feelings for him."

"All of this happened today?" Tia asked.

"No, it happened on Monday. Today he sort of apologized to me," I told her and she gave me a confused look. "Yeah, he told me that he should not have done what he did and we ended up getting into a discussion. He told me that he did not tell me to have feelings for him, I told him that he had to feel something for me." I stopped talking. I hated the next part and was still embarrassed by it.

"What happened after that?" Tia asked and I wished that Samantha could have been here. Samantha would have gone straight into the details, not allowing me to speak.

"He kissed me and I kissed him back." I was now crying. "He broke away, looked me in the eyes, and told me that he felt nothing." Tia wrapped her arm around me.

"It's okay."

"He felt nothing," I gasped.

"He's a Vampire, he's supposed to be heartless." Tia said with so much disgust.

"He's half-Vampire," I reminded Tia.

"I told you yesterday that I think he's more Vampire than a Protector." We stayed quiet for a minute, not so quiet because I was sobbing.

"I already am," I muffled. "Yesterday, you warned me that my feelings for him would grow and I could fall in love with him if I hadn't already...I already am--" I told her "--I'm in love with him."

"You are?" She asked and I thought about it.

"I think so, I don't know."

"You don't know?" She questioned me like I was crazy. Maybe I was.

"I've never had a boyfriend, I don't know what it feels like to be in love."

"How do you feel when he's around, how did you feel when he kissed you?" Tia asked.

"Alive," I breathed out.

"Can you think of him?"

"Why?"

"Just do it," she commanded and I did. Tia let out a gasp. "You really are. You're in love with him, your eyes glow just by thinking of him." She told me.

"How is that even possible. We reunited last month, kissed three times in total, and we've never been a couple." I was rummaging through my mind, trying to find an answer to that question.

"You don't have to be in a relationship to love someone," Tia told me and she was right.

"All my life, I've made fun of those foolish ordinaries for falling in love with their boyfriends or girlfriends after a couple of weeks of dating. Look at me, I've never even dated Nate and I am already in love. I am weak."

"You're not weak," Tia said. "Us Werewolves, Shape-Shifters, Wolf-shifters...whatever we call ourselves, have heightened feelings, that when we love, we really love."

"Can I still do something about it?" She knew what I was asking.

"You still have a little time." She said. "You just need to find someone, who is able to confuse your feelings for him. If you can find someone who is able to confuse your feelings for Nate before you transform, you should be good--" Tia said and I was relieved.

"I will." I promised.

After a while, Tia had to go. I walked her to her car and watched her drive away. "I heard you and Nate broke up," someone said. It was Edward. "It is so embarrassing when someone leaves you for an ex. It means that you could not help him move on." The door opened and Nate walked out.

"Who are you talking to?" He asked and saw me. I avoided his stare.

"Do you know I hate that bitch, Tessa." Edward told Nate.

"I know and I don't care."

"She's a Minder."

"So?"

"I prefer doggy here than your girlfriend," Edward pointed at me.

"I'm not a dog," I told him.

"Sorry, Werewolf." He apologized.

"I prefer the term Shape-Shifter or Wolf-Shifter," I said and started walking away.

"Whatever," I heard Edward said.

"She's a Minder too, you know." Nate said

"All I know is that I prefer a glimpse of my future over getting my brain fried." Edward said and for the first time this afternoon, I smiled.

The front door opened and I saw my mom walking out with a man who was probably in his early twenties. He was dark skinned with brown hair and eyes. He was an ordinary. I wondered how I didn't see him before. "Rosabelle, this is Joseph. Joseph, this is my daughter--Rosabelle." My mom introduced us, Joseph took my hand and kissed my knuckles. My mom had a huge smile on her face.

"You have a beautiful daughter, I can see why you added 'Belle' to her name." My mom and I giggled. I heard a scoff, I looked over and saw Nate's mouth gaped open, Edward was smiling.

"Thank you," my mom thanked him.

"Would you like to go to dinner sometime with me?" He asked me.

I looked at my mom and she gave me an encouragement nod. Joseph was definitely my key to confusion. "I would love to," I told him. A moment later, I heard a loud sound. I looked up and saw Edward. Nate was no longer with him.

"How about Saturday?" He asked.

"Sure," my mind was very far away. All I could think about was Nate, I really needed to stop thinking about him.

"Bye, Mrs. Foureau. Rosabelle, I'll see you on Saturday." I nodded my head.

He soon left. My mom and I walked back inside the house. I was about to heard upstairs when my mom stopped me. "What's going on between you and Nate?" My mom asked me in a curious voice.

"Nothing, mom."

"Tell me the truth, all of it." She demanded and I did. I told her everything that has been going on between me and Nate.

"He told me that he felt nothing," I finished.

"I'm so sorry." My mom told me. She felt pity for me.

"Me too, mom, me too." I said and went to my room. I noticed Nate sitting on his window sill, reading a book. He always loved to read. He looked up when I turned on the lights. I ignored him, grabbed my painting equipment, and started painting.

~~~

"Where were you first period?" Samantha asked. She was cornering me in my locker. I ditched my first-period class to go to the library. All we were doing in first period was reading Macbeth by Shakespeare and I hated Shakespeare.

"I was at the library," I responded.

"Why were you at the library?"

"I didn't want to be near Nate."

"Why?" She asked. I looked at her, her eyes were calculating me. I knew she was reading my mind. "I knew I should not have left you alone with him."

"I should have never followed him," I told her.

"I'm sorry," she said. It's okay. "Why are your eyes glowing?" She asked and I shrugged my shoulders. It's nothing. "You love him," she breathed out. I finished what I was doing at my locker and started walking away. "Wait, Rosabelle. Where are you going? We need to talk about this."

"No, we don't," I looked at her and bumped into someone. My things fell on the floor. I immediately bent down and started picking them up. Someone was also helping me pick things up. "Thank you--" I said, looking up.

I met gray eyes. "You're welcome," Nate said.

I quickly got up and left. I walked outside to the student parking lot. "Rosabelle, what are you doing?" Samantha called after me. I wanted to go home, I could not be at school right now. I opened the car door and Samantha shut it close. "Why?" Of course, she knew what I was thinking.

"Because of him."

"Look, I get it. You love him, he knows about your feelings for him, and he doesn't feel anything for you."

"Or cares," I cried. Samantha wrapped me in a hug.

"What's going on?" A voice asked. Samantha unhugged me and looked at Dylan.

"What are you doing here?" Samantha asked him.

"I had a doctor's appointment this morning, so I am late." He informed us. He observed me. "Why are you crying?" He asked and Samantha glared at him. "Rosabelle, why are you crying, did Nate hurt you again?" He asked me, ignoring Samantha's glare.

"What do you think?" I asked him and he nodded knowingly and stared at Samantha.

"What did he do?" He asked Samantha.

"He kissed her and told her that he felt nothing for her--" Samantha told him.

"He said that?" He asked in disbelief. "I will be right back--" he told us and walked away. Samantha and I followed him inside school.

"What are you doing?" I asked him. He kept looking straight ahead.

"I'm going to teach this asshole a lesson." This was not a good idea.

"Dylan, stop--" I called. He kept walking. "Dylan, he will hurt you."

"I don't care. No one hurts one of my friends and gets away with it--" he told me.

I told him, "If you go after him, you're the one who's going to get hurt...physically." Someone appeared in the hallway that we were in, it was Nate. We all looked uneasily at each other. A moment later, Dyan started to advance him.

"Dylan, you need to stop." Samantha started to panic.

Dylan did not listen and punched Nate in the face. Nate gave him a menacing look and I knew he was going to attack him. "Nate, don't." I pleaded. "Please, don't hurt him." Nate backed away, but Dylan did not.

"You asshole, why would you kiss her and tell her you felt nothing?" Dylan questioned.

Nate glared at me. "You told them?" He asked me. I looked away for a moment. I could feel his glare radiating toward me.

"Of course, she told us. We are her friends." Samantha scoffed at him. Nate approached me. Both Dylan and Samantha stepped in front of me.

"Stay away from her, you've already done enough damage." Dylan spat at him.

"Get out of my way." Nate warned them.

"No, we won't let you hurt her again--" Samantha told him.

Nate stared down at Dylan and Samantha. "I don't give a fuck about what you two fucking want--" Nate spat at them "--this is between me and Belle." He still called me 'Belle' why?

"She doesn't want to talk to you," Dylan said.

"I think she can speak for herself," Nate told them. They all looked at me.

"Don't call me that," I told Nate. "Don't call me 'Belle.'" He scoffed at me.

"I will call you whatever I want to call you," Nate told me. 'Of course,' I thought.

"I don't want you to call me that."

"I don't care about what you want." He looked at me and I looked back.

"You never care about me," I breathed out.

He looked at Dylan and Samantha."Leave," he told them.

"The last time I left you alone with her, you ended up hurting her." Samantha said.

"Leave!" He snarled at them.

They looked at me for guidance. I gave them a nod and they left. "Don't hurt me." I breathed out. A flash of hurt crossed his face. He started to advance me and I took steps back.

"I will never hurt you, I'm not a monster."

"Emotionally," I told him and he understood.

"I can't promise you that."

"Goodbye," I told him and started to leave. He took hold of my hand, sparks flew through me, our fingers were intertwined together.

"We need to talk," he said. I detached my hand from his hand and scoffed.

"That's exactly what you said last time."

"I know, but I'm not going to kiss you again--" he said and I felt disappointment. "I'm sorry...I should not have done what I did and said those words." He apologized.

"Yeah, you should not have, but you did." I looked at him straight in the eyes.

"I'm trying to apologize here," he told me in a tone of disbelief.

"Apologizing is not going to cure me," I told him.

"Cure you from what?" He demanded.

'My broken heart,' I thought and almost told him. "Don't worry about it." We gazed at each other for a minute.

"The least you can say is '\ accept your apology.'" He was gazing at me. His gray eyes were burning through mine.

"I accept your apology," I said and started walking away. I wished for him to stop me.

"Wait," he said and I stopped walking. "Whatever happens between us, stays between us. I don't want you to tell them everything--" he told me.

"I don't give a worth about what you want."

"I want us to be private."

"There is no 'us.'"

"Are you sure about that?" He asked.

We stared at each other for a moment. "I don't need to tell Samantha anything, she reads my mind and tells Dylan."

"Well, you need to control your friends next time, I won't be so gentle with Dylan next time."

"Is that a threat?" I asked him.

"Just a warning," he said and left.

CHAPTER TEN

"A warning?" Dylan repeated in disbelief.

We were in the parking lot, school had just ended. "Don't expect me to tell you two everything that happens between Nate and I anymore," I told them. They both gazed at me in disbelief. "He wants to keep us private."

"But there's no 'us' for you two," Samantha scoffed and I agreed.

"That's what I said and he asked me if I was sure about that."

"Maybe he secretly likes you," Samantha said. Dylan and I scoffed.

"He sure has a way of showing it," Dylan mocked.

"He sort of got mad when I agreed to go on a date with Joseph," I told them.

"Who's Joseph?" They both asked.

"The guy I'm going on a date with tomorrow," I informed them.

They looked at each other. "Can you give us details about him?" Samantha asked.

They both had a serious look on their faces. Geez, they needed to relax, it was just a date. Why were they protective all of the sudden. "He's black, in his twenties." I informed them.

"He's older than you?" Samantha gasped.

"Dude, relax. It's not like he's forty." I reassured her and she rolled her eyes.

"Why are you going on a date?" Dylan asked.

"Because I want to, I have the freedom to go out with someone."

"Are you even ready?" Samantha asked, looking serious. What was wrong with them.

"What do you mean?" I asked her.

"You still love Nate." She said.

"You are going to be leading Joseph on." Dylan said.

I looked at them in disbelief. "I'm not going to lead him on if I'm trying to move on from Nate," I angrily said.

"Rosabelle, you're in a state of disappointment, you've been rejected by Nate___" Samantha started.

"You have a broken heart to cure." Dylan added.

"I don't have a broken heart," I lied.

They both gazed at each other and shook their heads. "That totally explains the tears this morning," Samantha said with sarcasm.

"Rosabelle, you are in a vulnerable state right now, it's not good if you date someone right now." Dylan said and I got angrier. I really needed to get my anger in control. They were just being truthful.

"How dare you say that?" I spat at Dylan. His eyes widened and he had a look of disbelief on his face.

"Rosabelle, you need to listen to us--" Samantha said. I scoffed at her. "We are just looking out for you." Samantha tried to reassure me, but I could not be reassured.

"He's not," I pointed at Dylan.

"Why are you saying that?" Samantha asked. She was confused. I looked straight at Dylan.

"You are a Seeker, you should know what's going to happen to me if I don't try to move on."

"What is she talking about?" Samantha asked Dylan.

"But, it's already late, your eyes glow when you think of him--" Dylan said.

"No, it's not. I can confuse the feelings I have for Nate by going out with Joseph."

"What's going on?" Samantha asked.

"She has to date someone," Dylan told her. She was in a state of confusion. "If she doesn't move on or at least confuse her feelings for Nate, Rosabelle will go into a grave depression and might kill herself."

"What?" Samantha gasped and looked at me. I closed my eyes and looked down. "Did you know about this?"

"Kind of." I whispered.

"And you still did not prevent yourself?"

"You don't understand," I told her.

"No, I understand perfectly. You've been risking yourself over him." She said.

"Samantha__" Dylan warned.

"I found out too late." I told her.

"Even after you found out, you still wanted to know if he felt something for you."

"Of course I wanted to know--" I whispered "--Anyone would want to know."

"Not me--" she said "--he's a monster."

I felt so much anger when she said that, I wanted to slap her, but she was my friend, so I controlled my anger. "I have to go," I said through gritted teeth.

"Look, I'm sorry, but he does not even care about you. He throws you away like you're a piece of trash," Samantha said. My anger was now out of control, I advanced her. "Rosabelle, I just think that he's a waste of your time."

"Samantha, stop talking. You're pissing her off," Dylan told her. "She's transforming, she can't control her anger."

"Don't you think I know that?" I snarled quietly at her. "How dare you call him a monster."

"That's because he is," she said.

My teeth were hurting. I knew what was happening. "Rosabelle, you need to control yourself--" Dylan told me, but I ignore him.

"She needs to shut her mouth," I snarled at him.

Suddenly, I was pulled into a hug. My body ignited and I knew it was Nate. "We are surrounded by ordinaries, do you think it's a good idea to piss off a transforming Wolf-Shifter?" Nate asked. I knew he was addressing to Samantha...and glaring at her. "Leave."

"No, we're not leaving her alone with you--" Samantha protested.

"Why, because in your little head, you think I'm a monster?" Nate asked.

"Think?" Samantha asked. "I know you are." For some reason, I wanted to plunge myself on her. Nate pulled me closer to him.

"You two need to leave, especially you, Samantha--" Nate said. I knew Samantha was offended.

"Excuse you?"

"You're the one who's pissing her off," Nate said. A moment later, I heard them leaving. "You need to breathe," Nate whispered in a soft voice to me. I took deep breaths and was now calmed. "Are you okay?" He asked and I pushed him away.

"Of course not," I told him. "Like everyone else, she thinks of you as a monster."

"I should be the one angry, not you."

"I can't help it," I looked him in the eyes. He knew what I was saying.

"You need to go home," he said. He opened the door for me and I stepped in. He closed the door after me, but before I drove away, he tapped on my window. "Look, Belle. I know it's probably not a good time to say this, but we need to stay away from each other."

"Whatever you say, Nate--" I said and drove away.

~~~

"You look beautiful," Joseph greeted me.

We were in front of my house. "Thank you," I thanked him. He opened the door to his car for me and I stepped in. He drove us to a movie theater, that was not exactly my idea for a first date, but I was not complaining. We watched a comedic movie and I laughed so hard throughout it.

When the movie was over, he decided to drive me home. When we arrived home, he walked me over to my porch. "What's going on between you and him?" He nodded toward Nate who was sitting on his porch. Nate quickly looked up at us.

"Nothing."

"Is he an ex?"

"No."

"Does he like you?" He asked. That was too many personal questions for a first date.

"He's never shown an interest in me," I told him while looking at Nate.

"He was a bit pissed when you agreed to go on a date with me--" He said, remembering that evening.

"He's always pissed at something," I assured him.

Nate and I looked at each other, I could feel Joseph's gaze on me. "Your eyes are glowing," he said in wonder.

"They tend to glow in the dark." I closed my eyes for a moment and looked back at him. We said goodbye to each other and I walked into my house. My dad met me inside.

"How was your date?" He asked and I shrugged my shoulders. "Where did you two go?"

"The movies," I responded. My dad scoffed and rolled his eyes. He hated the idea of going to movies for first dates. "The movie was funny, so I had fun."

"I love comedic movies," my dad admitted.

"Who doesn't?"

~~~

I was on my way to my locker when I saw Samantha and Dylan already waiting for me. I quickly turned around and walked in a different direction. When the bell rang, I walked to class. Samantha was in her seat, I also saw Nate. I avoided both of their eyes on me and sat down quietly. We said nothing to each other for six minutes. "Rosabelle, can I talk to you?" Samantha asked.

"No, I'm trying to listen to the teacher--" I lied. The teacher was in his seat, grading our assignments quietly.

"He's not even talking," Samantha said.

"I don't want to talk to you," I told her. I knew I hurt her feelings.

"Look, I'm sorry that I overreacted. I had a best friend once who committed suicide. I'm not ready to lose you too because of him," Samantha said. Nate glanced over at me with confusion.

"What is she talking about?" Nate asked.

I just ignored him. "The fact that I could lose you to him made me so angry and I could not help myself to not call him and think of him as a monster." Samantha explained.

"You're thinking about suicide?" Nate gasped.

"No," I told him. At least not yet. "It's nothing like that."

"Yet," Samantha said.

"What is she talking about?" He asked.

"You won't understand," I told him.

"What won't I understand? The last thing I want is you committing suicide--" Nate said.

"I'm not talking to you," I said.

"You need to."

"No, I don't--" I told him "--we need to stay away from each other, remember?"

"Right now, we're sitting next to each other--" Nate said and I scoffed.

"Well, let's not talk to each other--" I said.

He kept his eyes on me. He could be so overwhelming. "Why didn't you tell him the truth?" He asked. "When Joseph asked you about your eyes, you lied." I looked at him, why did he care?

"Why do you care?"

"You should have told him the truth."

"Really, Nate. Are you even aware of the truth?"

"Of course, I am the reason your eyes glow--" Nate said and I scoffed at him.

"You won't be for long."

"Won't I?" He asked--looking at me, I looked back. His eyes were blue today. We gazed at each other for a while. I was lost in his eyes and he was lost in mine. "Your eyes get brighter for me every day," he softly whispered.

For the rest of the class we said no more. The day went fast and it was time to go home. "How was your date?" Dylan asked.

"It was okay." I said.

"Okay?" He repeated. "That's not good. Where did you two go?"

"Movies," I said.

"That is so clichée," Samantha said and we all agreed. "Did he kiss you?" Samantha asked.

"Don't you know already?" I asked her.

"No, you're blocking me--" Samantha said. I was confused, how was I doing that. I was not thinking about a lot of things.

"How is this even possible?" I asked them.

"Her specialty does not really work with Wolf-Shifters," Dylan told me.

"Why?"

"I don't know. Your venom can block any Minder's specialty for a week," Dylan said.

Both Samantha and I gasped. Samantha had drunk from my water bottle earlier today. "I drank from your water bottle." Samantha clasped her hand to her mouth.

"I forgot about that," Dylan said. "Your spits contain venom."

"That explains a lot, I'm not able to read what's on anyone's mind--" Samantha said.

"That's good," I said. "People deserve their privacy."

"No, they don't." She protested. "I can't do one week without my specialty."

"Yes, you can. Ordinaries do it all the time." Dylan said.

Samantha put her foot down. "I am not an ordinary, I am a Minder--" she fused "--can't this be cured?"

Dylan and I looked at each other. We knew the nurse could cure her, but Samantha needed to stop getting into people's head. "No." We both responded. We were terrible friends.

"What are you two thinking about?" Samantha asked and I smiled.

"This is going to be fun," I told Dylan. We both laughed at Samantha.

"You never answered my question--" Samantha said, several minutes later.

"No, I don't like the idea of kissing on first dates." I answered her question.

"Is he in college?"

"Yes, he goes to BSU." I told her.

"When is your next date?"

"Next Saturday," I answered her.

"Do you like him?" Dylan asked.

"He's okay," I said.

"Okay?" Samantha questioned. "That's not good."

"I just met him four days ago and we only had one date." Samantha and Dylan looked at each other. I knew they were thinking about Nate. "Nate and I are different. We go way back," I added.

"Oh, yes. That's right, you two had your first kiss with each other--" Samantha mocked.

"Shut up," I demanded in a light tone.

~~~

It has been two weeks since my first date and I started to like Joseph a little. We've only kissed one time and it was a disaster, it was just terrible. He was a good kisser, but to me, Nate was a hundred times better. Today, we were going on our fourth date, I had on shorts and a t-shirt. He was waiting for me in front of his car. "Hey," he advanced me and kissed me on the lips. I kissed him back, but I felt nothing.

I quickly broke away. "Hi," I greeted him back. I heard a soft chuckle, it was Nate. He was on his porch, reading a book. He was always reading a book.

"Are you ready?" Joseph asked. I quickly looked at him and smiled.

The date was fun, we went to a band concert, it was loud, and there was a huge crowd. I loved it. After that, we went to a small, cozy restaurant and ate dinner. "Joseph," a woman called and Joseph froze. She was a beautiful black girl.

"Shit," I heard Joseph mumbled under his breath.

"You must be his sister," she said to me. "It's a pleasure to finally meet you." I looked at her in confusion.

"You are mistaken," I said. "I 'm not his sister, I'm his date."

"What?" She asked and looked at Joseph.

"Natalie, you're not supposed to ask customers personal questions." Joseph told her in a low voice. What was going on with him, what was he on edge? So many questions were going through my mind.

"Sorry," Natalie apologized. Several seconds later, a different waiter came and took our requests.

"What was that about?" I asked. We were already in my house.

"It's nothing, don't worry about it--" he said agitatedly.

He did not want to talk about it, so I did not push him. He walked me to my front porch, he was about to kiss me when I stopped him. "I'm tired," I told him and went inside my house. Something was definitely wrong with Joseph.

~~~

On Sunday night, I sat on my window sill and gazed at the stars. I wanted to count them, but my mom once told me I would die if I did that. Haitians were superstitious about everything. "He's cheating on you," a voice said. I looked over and saw Nate sitting on his window sill. 'when did he get here?' I thought.

"What did you just say?"

"He's cheating on you," he repeated.

"How would you know?"

"I saw him in the park kissing another girl today," Nate confirmed. "I heard him say her name."

"I don't want to know," I lied. I needed to know.

"Her name is Natalie," he told me anyway. I gasped. I could not believe my ears.

"You're lying."

"I'm not," he said. I quickly took out my phone and dialed Joseph's number.

"Hi," he answered.

I walked out of my bedroom to get some privacy. "Are you cheating on me?" I asked.

"What?" He half-yelled. "Why would you ask that?"

"Nate saw you kissing Natalie in the park today," I told him. He was silent for a moment.

"She kissed me first and I pushed her away."

"You pushed her away?"

"Yes, I will never cheat on you." He promised. There was a question on my mind.

"Why would she kiss you?" I demanded. "What is she to you?"

"She is just a crazy ex." He tried to assure me, but I was not really assured.

I had more questions, but I didn't want to sound like the jealous girlfriend. "Okay, I'm sorry." I apologized and quickly hung up. I stormed to my window, Nate was still sitting on his window sill. "Don't you want to see me happy?"

"What?"

"He's not cheating on me, he pushed her away." I explained to Nate.

"Pushed her away or pulled her closer?" Nate asked.

"I believe him."

"Do you? Deep down you know I'm right," he said. "He's cheating on you, you are a second choice to him."

"I don't really care."

"Really? The Rosabelle I know will never want to be somebody's second choice," Nate said and my anger flared up.

"You don't know me that well--" I said "--I'm the one who's dating him, not you."

"I'm just looking out for you."

"I don't care," I half shouted at him. He looked surprised. "You're always telling me that I should mind my business. Well, Nate. You need to mind your business." I said and shut the window in his face.

~~~

We had no school today, so my dad and his pack thought it was a good idea to train me further. They wanted to see if I would transform today, so they were making me angry. A Wolf-Shifter kicked me and I flew out of the forest, in front of Nate's house. I looked up and saw him, Edward, and his mom watching with their mouth opened. Twenty Wolf-Shifters walked out of the forest and surrounded me. Two Wolf-Shifters kept whistling on some kind of whistle, they were brothers. "Stop it," I snarled at them.

"She needs to be angrier," my dad told them.

"Yes, leader--" One said and advanced me. His name was Louis. He picked me up by the throat and held me tight. He put a whistle on his mouth with his free hand and blew it at me. That made me angrier. I scratched him with my nails and managed to bite his hand. He groaned in agony. I kicked him in the stomach. The brothers were still whistling, I picked one up, and threw him against the other one with all my strength. Everyone gasped...shocked.

I was walking toward the one who first kicked me when I felt one of my bones snapped. I felt on the ground and screamed. All of the Wolf-Shifters were mumbling with excitement. Another bone snapped and another one. I dug my nails on the ground and looked at my dad. "Make it stop," I begged him.

"I can't, you're transforming--" he said and nodded at the Wolf-Shifter who had kicked me. He kicked me again and my spine snapped.

"AAH!" I screamed in agony and started crying. He was about to kick me again.

"Stop!" A voice interrupted. "You all need to stop." It was Nate.

My dad snarled and advanced him. "We are not stopping until I say so." My dad told him and stared at him with disgust.

"Your daughter is suffering. Can't you see how much pain she is in?" Nate asked.

"We've all gone through that pain and suffering," Tia said. "Now it's her turn."

"Nate," I gasped. "Help me." Nate made a move toward me and all of the Wolf-Shifters turned into huge wolves except my dad and Tia.

"Don't step any closer toward my daughter," my dad warned Nate in a low voice.

"She needs my help--" Nate protested, looking at me.

"You move one step, we attack--" my dad said.

The bones of my face were transforming. I felt like I was dying. "Aah!!" I screamed. They all looked at me in wonder. My vision became blurry, the last thing I saw was Nate before I passed out.

CHAPTER ELEVEN

I was really hot, my body felt gross, I was sweating. What was that smell? It smelled like a bunch of wet dogs. I knew it was not me. "Belle," I heard someone said my name. My body sprang alive, only Nate could do that. I opened my eyes and saw Nate leaning toward me. He smiled and I smiled back.

"You can leave now, Vampire. She's okay." A Wolf-Shifter said, glaring at Nate. Nate looked at him and glared. The Wolf-Shifter got a bit uncomfortable. I smiled, only Nate could do the glares. My heart started to pick up, Nate looked at me, and smiled.

"How about all of you--who is not my daughter and husband--get out of my house." My mom said loud and clear.

Everyone made way for Nate to get out first, some Wolf-Shifters snarled at him when he passed by and Nate hissed at them, making them all on edge. "Do you guys have to snarl at him?" I asked once Nate left.

"He's a bloodsucker," one said.

"He has not drink any blood apart from his own, how does that make him a bloodsucker?" They all got quiet for a moment.

"He will soon one day," my dad said.

"I don't think so."

"How would you know?" One asked.

"I'm a Seer," I explained. "I would know if he were to drink blood."

~~~

Today was Valentine's day. It was not really my favorite holiday, since I've never received flowers apart from my dad who made a deal with me years ago. I found a rose in my locker with a note,

Love you,

Dad.

I smiled. I put the rose and the note back in my locker and walked to class. Some girls in the class were receiving flowers and kept giggling like fools. Samantha received a yellow flower from Dylan. Tessa was upset about something, "Where's my rose?" She demanded Nate and he rolled his eyes at her.

"It's here," Nate said when a boy walked in with a yellow rose, the boy handed Tessa the flower.

"What is this?" She demanded Nate. "We are together, you're supposed to give me pink roses. This--" she waved the flower in his face "--is for friendship."

"And that's what we will be from now on," Nate said and Tessa gasped loudly in shock.

"What are you saying?"

"Look, I told you that I would give it a try and I did, but I'm over it...I'm over you--" Nate said, looking at her straight in the eyes.

"You're breaking up with me on Valentine's day?" She gasped.

"I didn't want to lead you on any longer."

"Is Rosabelle here?" Someone interrupted.

"I'm Rosabelle," I told him. He came toward me and handed me four bouquets of roses, a total of one hundred. Everyone in the room gasped. "Are those for me?" I had a huge smile on my face, even Nate was smiling. I looked for a note, but I could not find one. "Where's the note?"

"He wants you to figure him out," the boy said and left. Who could it possibly be?

~~~

I managed to open my bedroom's door, I put the bouquets on my bed. My mom came into the room and gasped. "Joseph?"

"I assume." I took out my phone and called Joseph. He picked up the phone. "Hi, I wanted to thank you for the roses."

"What roses?"

"Today I received roses, it's Valentine's day--" I reminded him. I was holding my breath.

"They aren't from me, I don't do roses--" he told me. Why am I going out with him? I thought.

"Okay, bye." I hung up on him. I looked at my mom, who was waiting for me to say something. "It wasn't him."

"They could be from your dad," my mom said. "Is there a note?"

"No, I could not find any--" I told her.

My mom stared at the bouquets thoroughly. "There's one right there," she said. "You just needed a second pair of eyes." She handed me the Note.

I hope you're happy.

The one your eyes

glow for.

I gasped.

"Nate." I told my mom and quickly ran out of my house and barged inside his house without knocking. Nate opened his bedroom door before I had a chance to barge in there too. I handed him the note.

"It took you long," he said.

"Are you playing games with me?" I asked him and he scoffed.

"No."

"Why did you give me those bouquets?"

"I wanted to give you bouquets."

"I'm dating someone."

"Who did not bother to give you one rose," Nate laughed at me.

"He didn't have to."

"Really?"

"He's not romantic," I told him.

"With you, but not with Natalie."

"He's not cheating on me."

"You can be so naive," he said. I scoffed at him and started to leave__

"Where are you going?" He asked.

For some reason, I felt the need to tell him. "Joseph is picking me up at six to go to a Valentine party."

"Where?"

"I'm not telling you."

"Don't trust him," Nate warned. Whatever. I started to leave again, "Why are you dating him?"

"Excuse you?"

"He's an ordinary."

"So?"

"You know what always happens," he reminded me.

"I'll be careful."

"You can't keep your abilities a secret from him, he has to know--" Nate said.

"Nor can I tell him."

"That's why you need to break up with him." Nate said and I understood what he was implying.

"You just want us to break up."

"I don't want you to kill him," Nate shouted. "I'm part Protector and my job is to protect ordinaries from Supernaturals.

"I'm not going to kill him."

"You can either tell him or break up with him."

"If I tell him, he will die--" I told him. Supernaturals weren't allowed to tell ordinaries about themselves because the ordinaries would die.

"Break up with him." I glared at him for a moment before turning away.

"I have a party that I need to get ready to," I told him.

"If you don't break up with him by tomorrow, you will have Protectors to deal with." He warned.

I quickly faced him and advanced him. "How dare you, this is my life, I can be with anyone I want." I snarled at him. My anger was out of control. No Supernaturals who got involved with humans got off okay with the Protectors, their methods of punishment were worse than anyone could ever imagine.

"We, Supernaturals should never get involved with ordinaries--" he said "--your parents could get punished too...because they know Joseph is an ordinary, and they are still allowing you to go out with him." Nate explained.

"I have a party to attend," I said and left.

~~~

Joseph kissed me on the lips, but I quickly broke away. We were at the party, the place was crowded, the music was loud, it was hurting my eardrums. "Why won't you kiss me back?" He asked. My body ignited. I quickly looked at the doorway and saw Nate. He was looking around and his eyes fell on me.

"Let's dance," I demanded Joseph and we started dancing. We danced for thirty minutes, I was not tired, but I was hot. Joseph was sweating.

"I'm tired. Let's do something else," he said.

"Like what?"

"Let's go upstairs," he smiled at me.

I knew what he wanted to do. People always went upstairs during parties to do one thing, get kinky. "And do what?" I asked him, searching for a way out. I saw Nate.

"You know." He smiled.

"I don't want to."

"Why not?"

"You're not special to me."

"People do it just to get it over with," he pressured me. What was wrong with him. We've only dated for a month and he wanted to have sex. He was not even my boyfriend. We've never made ourselves official.

"I don't want that."

"Why not?" He asked.

At this point, he was really pissing me off. I looked at him for a really long time. I was not even sure if I even liked him one bit, he was not my type, he did not give me flowers for Valentine, he really was a waste of my time. "Are you aware that I'm a minor?" I reminded him. I wanted to let him down easy.

"No one has to know."

"I don't want to date you anymore," I told him flatly.

"What did you just say?" He asked, glaring at me. I glared back at him.

"You're just a waste of my time," I told him.

"Bitch, you better watch how you speak to me--" he spat with such menace...I slapped him. "You ungrateful bitch," he said and pushed me against the wall.

Half a second later, Nate attacked him. I quickly recovered myself and pulled Nate off him. "The next time you touch her, I'll cut your hands." Nate warned and guided me outside to his car. "Get in the car," He commanded. I looked around, I wanted some fresh air, I looked back at Nate.

"No, I'll walk." I told him. He advanced me.

"Get. In. The. Fucking. Car. Now." He quietly hissed at me.

"Okay," I told him and quickly got in the car.

After fifteen minutes of driving, he parked in his driveway. "I'm glad you took my warning and broke up with him--" he said after he turned off the ignition.

"You could have killed him when you attacked him--" I said quietly, looking at him.

"So?" He asked. "He had his hands on you."

"Aren't you part Protector. I thought Protectors were supposed to protect ordinaries," I told him. He quickly gazed at me and I gazed back. This afternoon, you threatened to expose me to the Protectors."

"I would have never done that, I just wanted you to break up with him."

"Are you happy now?"

"I am," he smiled. He was extremely satisfied.

"Why did you want me to break up with Joseph?" I asked him. My breath was stuck in my throat.

"I already told you," he said quietly.

"Tell me the real reason," I demanded.

"I don't have to."

"Do you ever?" I quickly got out of his car and walked to my house.

"Rosabelle," Nate called. A moment later, he turned me around and kissed me fully on the lips. I automatically kissed him back. His hands were gripping my waist, pulling me closer. My hands were on his cheeks. He slowly pulled away. "I want us back together." Of course, he always thought of me as his girlfriend when we were kids. "Let's go out tomorrow."

"Okay," I breathed out and he smiled.

"I can't wait," he laid a kiss on my forehead and left.

CHAPTER TWELVE

Why are you smiling?" My mom asked when I got inside. I had a huge smile on my face. "Did you and Joseph have fun?" She asked and my smile disappeared.

"I dumped him."

"Why, what happened?"

"He wanted to have sex," I responded and she scoffed with anger.

"That bastard."

"I never really liked him, he didn't give me flowers today and he was cheating on me." I told her.

"He was cheating on you?"

"Remember the woman who interrupted our date?" My mom nodded. "Nate saw him and her kissing," I told her. We stayed quiet for a minute.

"How did you get home?" She asked. 'oh, oh.' I thought and walked away.

"I got a ride."

"With who?"

"Someone."

"Rosabelle," she warned.

"Nate," I told her.

She followed me all the way to my bedroom. "The one who gave you one hundred roses," she acknowledged and I rolled my eyes. I knew where she was getting at.

"Yes, that one."

"What's going on between you two?" My mom asked.

"We are really confusing," I told her.

"How come he was at the party?" My mom asked.

"I don't know, mom. I'm just glad he was there." I told her.

My mom was calculating me. "Did something happen between you two tonight?" She asked and I froze. I could never tell my mom that Nate asked me out and I agreed because she would automatically tell my dad and he would get angry and maybe rip Nate's head off.

"Something always happens," I told her and she nodded. She did not need to know the whole truth.

~~~

"Where are we going?" I asked Nate. We were walking deep inside a forest.

"We are going to see your species," he responded. what? "You'll see." We walked for another twenty-five minutes before we arrived at a clearing. "Over there," Nate nodded. I looked over and saw a pack of Wolves. There were at least thirty of them, I gasped. Little cubs were playing around. In a moment, they all advanced me, even the cubs. Nate kept his distance.

The Wolves circled me and stayed immobile. Two Wolves and three cubs broke the circle and advanced me. One of them was the alpha, his mate, and cubs. They kneeled in front of me and all the Wolves in the circle began kneeling. "Wow," I gasped. Nate was looking at me with so much awe. I picked up one of the little cubs, he was adorable. "Nate, come hold one."

"No, I'm good."

"Come on," I approached him and handed over the pup. Nate eyed me. "See, it's not that bad." I smiled at him. He carried the small Wolf in an uncomfortable way. We both sat down on the grass and he let the pup go.

"It's nice here," he said after a moment of silence.

"Do you come here often?"

"Yes, this place help me escape the real world." He told me. I gazed at him.

"You brought me to your escape place," I whispered.

He smiled and looked at me thoughtfully. "Yes, and I wanted our 377th date to be with your species--" he told me.

"Our what." I asked, shocked.

"When we were little, we had playdates every day for a year and eleven days." He told me.

"I remember." I smiled at him. "Thank you for bringing me here," I thanked him.

"It's better than the movies, right?" He asked.

He knew about my first date with Joseph. "The movies, that's cliché...this--" I looked around "--is original." I told him.

"So you like it?"

"I'm in love," I told him.

He smiled and pulled me closer him. He kissed me softly on the lips, I kissed him back with the same softness. A second later, he slowly broke away. "I want to race you," he told me. I stared at him.

"You know I'll win."

"I know, but I've always wanted to race someone with natural speed." I took off my shoes, Nate stared at me with a questioning look. "Why do Wolf-Shifters always have to run barefoot?"

"We love the feeling of the ground underneath our feet when we run," I told him and he nodded.

"Are you ready?" I turned the questions back at him. He softly chuckled and sprinted with full speed, leaving me behind. He was such a cheater.

"Hey!" I yelled and sprinted after him. The ground felt so good underneath my feet, I was running fast, probably the fastest I ever ran. I saw Nate ahead of me and quickly ran past him in a blur. I stopped running when I was out of the forest. Nate came out with a grin on his face, moments later.

"That was awesome," he said.

"You cheated."

"You still won."

"Exactly, you should be ashamed of yourself." I joked. His eyes twinkled.

"Ashamed?" He pretended to be offended. "You may be faster, but I'm stronger...do you remember what happened last time we ran into each other? You were the one impacted, I was fine." He was totally bragging. I rolled my eyes at him. "Are you rolling your eyes at me?"

"No," I smiled.

"Oh, Rosabelle. You and your sarcasm." He chuckled. I had no comebacks for him today. I gazed at him with wonder. I had not seen this side of him for a while. "Why are you looking at me like that?"

"You are happy today," I told him and he smiled even more. My heart picked up.

"Am I not always happy?" He asked and I laughed at him. If he only knew.

"No, you're always pissed at something--" I told him and he laughed.

"Really?"

"Yeah and you always glare at people," I added and he scoffed like I was bluffing.

"Am I glaring at someone right now?" He asked and I looked at him.

"No, you're smiling." I smiled.

He slowly advanced me and pulled me closer to his body. "You're making me happy," he said and was about to kiss me when my phone rang. I looked at the caller ID, it was my dad.

"It's my dad," I told Nate. "He's probably wondering where I am."

"Does he know about us?" Nate asked.

I looked at him like he was crazy. "Of course not," I told him. My dad would have Nate's head hanging from his mouth if he ever found out. The thought of Nate without a head gave me chills.

"Does your mom know?"

"No, I can never tell her."

"Why? She does not hate me."

"She tells my dad everything. If she ever knows about us, she will automatically go to my dad and tell him." I informed him. "Does your mom know?" I asked Nate. He quickly glanced at me and smiled.

"She saw us kissing yesterday."

"Oh, my God." I said, embarrassed. "Is she okay with me?" I asked nervously.

"Are you kidding, she's more than okay with you." Nate assured me and I relaxed.

"Did your family like you and Tessa together?" I asked. I already knew Edward hated her.

"They all hated her, they thought of her as an abomination." He told me and we both laughed.

His family actually went that far. "They went that far." I laughed.

"Yes." He laughed with me. "You are part Wolf-Shifter, Tessa is pure Minder...they hated her, especially Edward." 'what about Edward?' "She used her specialty on him," Nate answered my unspoken question."On thanksgiving," Nate quickly added. My eyes widened.

"What did he do?"

"He threw the whole turkey on her face and knocked her out," Nate told me. We went into silence for a moment before we cracked up with laughter.

~~~

"Where were you?" My dad asked as I walked inside the house. I looked at him,

"Out."

"Where."

"In the forest."

"What were you doing in the forest?" My dad asked.

He was asking way too many questions. "Why are you asking me so many questions?" I demanded him with curiosity. Did he know bout Nate and I? No, he could no have.

"I am your father, I need to know where you are in case of something happens."

"Like what?"

"Your transformation, you will need someone like me to be there with you or you might get out of control and kill someone." My dad said. I understood what he was saying.

"I was hanging out with Wolves and their pups," I told him half the truth.

"You were?" He asked in disbelief. "They're still out there." I nodded. "Did they kneel in front of you?" My dad asked and I smiled at the memory.

"Yes, it was magical." I told my dad and he smiled.

"They only do that to leaders or future leaders," my dad informed me.

I looked at him in shock. "Really?" I asked and I smiled.

"Looks like you're going to be the leader of the pack after all." My dad patted me on the back and left. Being the leader meant I would transform, transforming meant that Nate and I would be over. All my life, I've dreamed about my transformation, but now, I was not sure about it anymore.

CHAPTER THIRTEEN

"My specialty is back," Samantha announced and I froze. We were all in the cafeteria, eating lunch. I have not told Samantha and Dylan about Nate and I being together.

"It's back?" Dylan asked in a disapproving tone.

Samantha looked quizzically at him. "Why are you disappointed?" Samantha asked.

"Because you're going to be in everyone's privacy," Dylan said. It was the truth.

"No one deserves privacy, I've missed so much in life already." She said and observed Dylan. "Stop blocking me."

"Stop trying to read my mind," Dylan said. Samantha sighed and looked at me.

"How was your weekend?"

"It was good," I told her.

"How's everything with Joseph?"

"We broke up."

"When?"

"On Valentine's day."

"Why didn't you tell us?" Dylan asked.

"I'm telling you two now."

"Why did you break up with him," Samantha asked.

"He wanted to sleep with me."

"You're a minor, that's illegal." Dylan stated.

"He told me that no one would have to know." I informed them while shaking my head.

"What a pig," Dylan mumbled.

"Are you okay?" Samantha asked.

"I'm glad it's over."

"Why, you wanted this?" Dylan reasoned with me.

"I got a warning."

"You got a warning?" They both repeated.

"I should have never gotten involved with an ordinary," I told them.

They had their mouths gaped open. "That was one of the reasons we did not want you to go out with Joseph." Samantha acknowledged Dylan and herself. Dylan had a look of confusion on his face.

"Protectors don't warn," he said.

"Nate felt the need to warn me."

They both gasped. Samantha stared at me and her eyes widened. "You two are together now." She eyed me. "Why didn't you tell us?"

"You called him a monster."

"I apologized, I don't know about Dylan." Samantha threw Dylan under the bus.

"I never called him a monster," Dylan said.

"And you never apologized," I told her.

"Yes, I did."

"To me, but not to him."

"Oh," she said. "Can you apologize for me?"

"No, do it on your own." I pressured her. She looked around the cafeteria.

"I don't see him."

"He's in the library," I informed her.

"I'll apologize after school."

"How about you do it now?" Dylan suggested.

"Fine." Samantha sighed and got up.

We followed her to the library. Nate was reading a book. He looked up and smiled when he saw me, but his smile soon faded when he saw who was with me. "We're the reason his smile faded." Dylan whispered to Samantha. She ignored him.

"Nate," Samantha began. Nate looked at her. "I'm sorry for thinking of you, and calling you a monster."

"I accept your apology." Nate accepted her apology.

Samantha looked at Dylan and smiled. "It's your turn."

"I never called him a monster."

"No, but you warned him to--and I quote, 'stay away from Rosabelle.'"

"So did you."

"I apologized."

"For something else," Dylan said. A moment later, he gazed at Nate. "I'm sorry." Dylan observed me for a moment. "Were you the one who gave Rosabelle one hundred roses?"

Nate stared blankly at him, he was not going to say anything. He wanted us to be private. Samantha glanced at me and read my mind. She gave Dylan a nod and looked at Nate.

"That was very...HUMAN of you." She smiled and I laughed. Samantha was too much. Samantha looked at me in confusion. "Why are you laughing?"

"You don't even know." I made a mockery of her.

"Let's go," she demanded and dragged me outside of the library. "I still can't believe this...he looked at me--" Samantha whispered. Dylan and I looked at each other in confusion. "He didn't glare at me," she said. "He always glares at me."

"Maybe he ran out of glares," Dylan said and I smiled. I knew the real reason.

~~~

"I don't want to do any more training," I told Tia. We were in my room.

"Why not?"

"Because I'm prepared now."

"What about your anger?"

"I can control it now."

"But you won't be able to control it when you transform."

"Then I'll resume my training," I assured her.

"That works." She was assured. "How's your appetite?"

I cringed at her question, my appetite was out of control. "It's like I'm on my period all the time," I said. She gave me a look. "I eat a lot when I'm on my period."

"You're like my sister, you can never trust her with food." Tia laughed.

"I'm hungry." I laughed.

"Me too," she said.

We went downstairs to get something to eat. We settled down with ice cream. In the middle of licking ice cream, her brain froze and I laughed. "Wolf-Shifters can have brain-freeze?" I asked her with wonder.

"We are humans," she told me. "We're just not ordinaries."

"We are so much better," I said. Wolf-Shifters had speed, strength, senses.

"Speaking of ordinaries, what's going on between you and Joseph, I heard you dumped him."

"He was a pig."

"Most ordinaries are pigs," she laughed. "But that's not the reason you dumped him, not really."

"I had to break up with him...I didn't want to deal with the Protectors."

"We cannot be punished by the Protectors," Tia informed me. "Not like the others." What did she mean? "Unlike other Supernaturals, we get a warning." She informed me and I rolled my eyes.

"That's what I got."

"Oh,"

"Why are we treated differently?"

"We protect humans from Vampires," she said. "Vampires come out at night and feed on humans and we hunt them down," Tia informed me.

"What do you do after you hunt them down?" I asked her. I already knew the answer to that.

"We rip their heads off."

"What about half-Vampires?" I asked.

She observed me for a moment. "They are okay as long as they're not feeding on humans," Tia told me.

"What about Supernaturals?"

"We don't care if they are feeding on Supernaturals, as long as they're not feeding on Wolf-Shifters."

"What about half Wolf-Shifters?"

"Half or pure...you're still a Wolf-Shifter. The rules apply." She informed me. We ate ice cream in silence for a minute. "Is there something going on between you and Nate?" My heart picked up.

"No, why would you ask that?"

"Your questions interested me," she said. "Are you sure there is nothing between you and Nate?"

"Yes." I told her, looking down. I didn't want her to see my eyes glow.

"What are you going to do now?" Tia asked after a moment, I finally looked at her. "Are you going to date someone new to confuse your feelings with Nate?" She asked and I immediately shook my head. "Why not?"

"I don't want to," I told her. I was already dating the person I loved, the one my body ignited for, the one my eyes glowed for. I did not want to date anyone who was not him.

"Are you aware of the consequences?"

"I am, I just don't care."

"How can you say that?"

"I'm happy with my life right now," I told her and she scoffed at me.

"Well, you won't be for long."

"The only thing that matters is that I'm happy now," I told her. "I am living my life in the present, I'll worry about the future when it comes."

"Then date someone in the present," she pressured me. I smiled at her.

"I am," I told her and quickly shut my mouth. What was wrong with me?

"You are?"

"No!" I half-shouted, hoping she would not believe what I had just said.

"You just said you were," she said, advancing me. She looked at me with her quizzical eyes. "Who?" I was panicking once again, but I had to tell her something.

"It really doesn't matter."

"Who?"

"Me?" I said in a questioning way.

"Yes, you."

"No, I mean, I'm dating myself." I informed her. She stared at me with a blank face. "Have you ever heard of the saying 'me, myself, and I?'" I asked her. She looked at me like I was stupid. "A lot of people are doing that, it's a form of therapy." I told her.

"Only ordinaries do therapy."

"Well, I'm happy now."

"You are happy?"

"Yes," I told her. She did not have to know that Nate was the reason for my happiness.

CHAPTER FOURTEEN

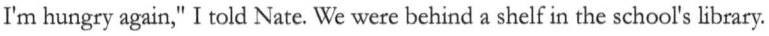

I'm hungry again," I told Nate. We were behind a shelf in the school's library.

"You just ate."

"I'm always hungry nowadays," I told him.

"That's because you're transforming," He said. He was playing with my earlobe. I scolded at him to stop. "I forgot. Wolves are sensitive with their ears," Nate mocked and I pushed him playfully.

"Shut up," I said and he attacked my lips. I kissed him back, my arms were around his neck, his arms were around my waist. We were so caught up in the kiss, we weren't aware of anything.

"There you are." Samantha and Dylan startled us.

Nate and I let go of each other and glared at them. "What are you two doing here?" I asked.

"Looking for you," they both responded.

"You've seen me, now go--" I told them.

I wanted to kiss Nate again...badly. He was my fuel and my body needed it...desperately. Samantha's mouthed gaped open, she was obviously reading my mind. "Dylan, let's go." Samantha gave him a nod for him to follow her. A moment later, they left. I smiled at Nate.

"Now, where were we?" I asked playfully.

"We were doing this," he pulled me toward him. We were about to resume kissing____

DUH

The bell rang.

"Let's ditch third period," Nate suggested.

"I can't, I have a test." I told him and left.

The day went fast, it was already time to go home. I was standing by my car, talking to Samantha and Dylan. "Does your dad know about you two?" Dylan asked and I gave him a look. "What about your mom?"

"She tells my dad everything, so no."

"So, you're secretly with him--" Samantha stated. I thought about it for a moment.

"Not really, you two and his mom know." I told them and Samantha scoffed at me.

"His mom knows and yours doesn't," Samantha scolded.

I felt bad a bit. "His mom saw us kissing," I informed them. We stayed quiet for a few moments.

"Are you ever going to tell them?" Dylan asked.

I had to tell my parents one day. I could never keep Nate and I a secret for long. "Of course I'm going to tell them...one day...not now." I said.

"When you tell your dad--" Dylan began "--make sure Nate is far away." Samantha asked him 'why.' "He will rip Nate's head off," Dylan told her. Samantha looked at me.

"Wolves have a thing for having their prey by the neck," I told her.

"What is this...*Twilight?*" She asked.

We both looked at her in confusion. "Do I glow in the sun to you?" Nate came behind Samantha, making her scream.

"You're half," Samantha said.

"In the real world, Vampires can only come out in the day eight times a year--" Nate scoffed at her.

"Do they glow?"

"We are not in *Twilight*," I told her.

Nate and I looked at each other, keeping our distances. "Why are you two acting weird?" Samantha asked. I looked around the parking lot. There were Wolf-Shifters around us, keeping an eye on me. Samantha understood, she got out her phone and texted Dylan.

"That explains the library," Dylan said. I stared at Nate, we had our acting faces on.

"What are you still doing here, are you looking for blood?" I asked Nate.

"No, I just wanted to see if you're smelling like a wet dog already." He said and left. I tried hard to contain my smile. Samantha and Dylan were amused.

"I have to go," I told them.

"Already?" Samantha asked.

"I have to study for my Economics class," I told them. I got into my car and drove away. When I arrived at my house, I saw Edward on my porch. I rolled my eyes and got out of my car. What did he want? "What do you want, Edward?"

"I heard you and Nate are together now--" He stated, approaching me.

"Yeah."

"Listen to me, Wolf-Shifter--" He spat and pointed a finger at me "--if you ever hurt or try to hurt my little cousin...you will have me to deal with."

"I'm not afraid of you," I told him.

"You should be," he warned. Anger rose through me. "I'm a Protector, don't make me punish you."

'That's it,' I thought. I had enough of his snarky comments. I pushed him with all my strength, he flew twenty yards away from me. "I'm a Wolf-Shifter, don't make me rip your head off--" I warned him. He quickly got up and tackled me to the ground. My teeth turned into canines and I snarled at him.

"If you hurt Nate, I'll make sure your canines are removed--" he warned. My instincts kicked in, I sunk my canines into his neck. He groaned loudly in pain.

"Rosabelle," someone called. I quickly let Edward go and looked at the direction of the voice, it was my dad. Some of the pack members appeared behind him, they were coming out of the forest. A moment later, Nate appeared and immediately reached for Edward, but stopped when he saw blood on his neck.

"What's going on?" Nate asked, looking at me.

"He tackled me," I told him.

"That's because you attacked me!" Edward shouted.

"Why would you attack him?" Nate asked.

"He was warning me."

All of the Wolf-Shifters started mumbling. "Why would you warn her?" My dad asked Edward. "She broke up with the ordinary." Nate glared at Edward and gave him a silent warning.

"I didn't know that," Edward said. "But your daughter bit me, she had no right."

"She is a transforming Wolf-Shifter...she can't control her anger," my dad defended me.

"She needs to control herself...before she makes an ordinary her victim."

"She will never cross that line," my dad assured Edward.

"She better not or she will be punished," Edward warned. My dad and Nate glared at him.

"He threatened to remove my canines," I said out loud. "Can he do that?" All of the Wolf-Shifters snarled at Edward.

"No more canines will be removed from this day--" my dad began "--if a Protector removes a Wolf-Shifter's canines, especially my daughter's...we will go to war. Go inform your fellow Protectors."

"We will have allies," Edward said.

"You mean Vampires," my dad spat and looked at Nate. Nate looked at me. "We will have Minders on our side." My dad then dragged me inside the house. "I can't stand them, thinking they are better than other Supernaturals."

"I'm glad you bit a Protector," a Wolf-Shifter said, Louis. He was holding Tia's hand. I never knew she had a boyfriend.

"I wasn't trying to, my instincts took over--" I told them and they all smiled.

"Why do we always go for the neck?" Tia asked.

"Because the neck holds the head," my dad responded and we all laughed.

~~~

I walked into the library, Nate had ditched first period. I saw him behind a shelf, reading a book. He looked up and saw me. "Hey," I greeted him. He did not greet me back. I sat down across from him. "Why did you skip class?"

"Why did you attack Edward?" He asked me instead.

"He warned me."

"What was his warning?"

"You don't know?"

"He would not tell me."

"He warned me that if I hurt or tried to hurt you...I would have him to deal with, that he would punish me." I told Nate.

He closed his eyes for a moment. "I'm sorry." He apologized and looked at me. "But you should not have attacked him."

"I could not control myself."

"You need to--" he said "--Edward was being protective."

"I know, but he did not have to threaten my canines--" I told Nate.

"And you should not have bitten him," Nate said. We stayed in silence for a moment, just staring at each other.

"Is he okay?"

"He is a Protector, he heals fast." Nate said. "You need to apologize to him." I looked at him like he was crazy. "He'll apologize to," Nate assured me.

"He's the only one who needs to apologize," I told him and he stared at me. "He was wrong."

"You were both wrong," Nate firmly said. "You both did bad things to each other...you bit him."

"I__"

"He's my cousin, you're my girlfriend. You two are my only best friends," Nate began. My heart picked up, he thought of me as his best friend and girlfriend. "I don't want to choose between you two."

"You won't," I assured him. "I'll apologize."

"Thank you," he sighed in relief. He looked at me for a long time. "Breathe." what? "Your heart is beating fast...the faster it beats, the more blood, it's pumping--" Nate whispered.

"Do you want to taste my blood?" I asked him and he gasped. I was offering him my blood.

"Are you offering me your blood?" He asked and I nodded. "I'm not allowed to taste a Wolf-Shifter's blood," Nate reminded me.

"We will keep it between us," I told him and he gave me a look.

"And Samantha and Dylan--" he added and I laughed.

"You have a point."

"When I was a little boy, I had this fantasy that my first time drinking blood would be special." Nate told me and I stared at him.

"Really?"

"Yes."

"Whose blood did you imagine?" I asked.

He looked at me and shrugged. "I can't recall," he said. I did not believe him, but I was not going to pressure him.

"Do you have a weakness for blood?" I asked him.

He looked away for a second. "Somedays, but I always manage to control my hunger--" he told me. He was telling me a lot, his usual self would have told me to mind my business.

"How?"

"I eat human food and sometimes taste my own blood--" he said. I imagined him tasting his blood.

"Does it taste good?" I asked and he laughed.

"Bad enough to turn off my hunger," he told me and I joined in his laughter.

~~~

"I am so sorry for threatening you," Edward apologized. He was in the living room of Nate's house.

"I'm sorry for biting you."

"You mean for sinking your canines into my flesh?" Edward asked.

"You healed pretty quick," I told him and he laughed.

He looked at Nate for a moment. "I want to talk to Rosabelle." Edward told Nate. Nate looked at him, unsure. "Don't worry."

"One minute," Nate told him and gave us privacy.

Edward and I glanced at each other before he spoke. "I never warned Tessa about hurting Nate," Edward began. I looked at him.

"Why me?"

"You hurt him once already," he said. I went immobile.

"Me...when?"

"You broke his heart when you left to Oregon, he cried over you." Edward told me. My heart broke.

"He did."

"Yes. You are the only girl he ever cried about."

"I am."

"I just don't want you to hurt him again."

"I don't want to hurt him either," I assured him.

Nate soon appeared, he smiled at me. "How do you feel bout a game of Backgammon?" He asked and I smiled.

"I feel very strongly about that," I told him. He knew Backgammon was my favorite game to play.

We played Backgammon for a while. Nate won one time and I won three times. Edward was making fun of Nate because Nate was having a hard time to beat me. "Where's your game, Nate." I mocked and he playfully glared at me.

"I'm not feeling it today," he responded and I laughed.

"Do you ever feel it when you play with me?" I mocked him.

Edward laughed. "Are you going to take that?" He asked Nate. Nate looked at me, he had a malicious smile on his face.

"No, I'm not--" he said. 'oh, oh.'

CHAPTER FIFTEEN

Nate shuffled one more time and got double ace. He got up, threw his hands in the air, claiming his victory. Edward was laughing so hard. "Where's your game, Belle?" Nate mocked me, throwing my words at me, Edward laughed harder.

"You got lucky."

"Luck?" He questioned. "I don't call that 'luck.' I won because I'm smart and was calculating your moves."

"What?"

"You see, I know your every move and how you think when you're playing Backgammon." He started.

"And you let me won three times?" I rolled my eyes and scoffed at him.

"I told you, I wasn't feeling it."

"Right."

"You are the most competitive person I know," Nate said and I laughed.

"Are you hearing yourself?" I asked.

He smiled and took my hand. "I have something I need to show you in my room," Nate said and Edward laughed. Nate and I glanced over at him.

"Have fun, you two, but not too much fun." Edward warned. "I am too young to be an uncle," Nate glared at him. Edward quickly went quiet. Nate guided me upstairs to his room. He pulled me toward him and kissed me on the lips. I curled my fingers on his shirt and kissed him back. In a couple of seconds, I fell on the bed, he climbed on top of me and started kissing me again. I ran my hands down his spine, through his shirt.

A moment later, he took off his shirt. I gazed at his chest, open mouthed. He was pretty muscular. He chuckled lightly at my reaction. Without any thought, I reached my hands and guided them down and up his chest, tracing his muscles and abs with my fingers. I looked him in the eyes and tugged his nipples gently with my fingers, he looked surprised when I did that. I could not help myself from giggling.

Nate was smiling heartily from ear to ear, he was so handsome when he smiled. He could light up my world for eternity with his smile.

He placed a hand on my lower jaw, tilted my head back, and kissed me again. Fire ignited throughout my body. My heart was pacing. I pushed him onto the bed, climbed on top of him. He sat up, so now I was on his lap, my legs around his waist. I stared into his eyes, he had a look of hunger in them.

We kissed each other on the lips for a while before he started laying kisses on my neck. Three seconds later, I felt sharp things sliding on my neck. It was his fangs, I was a bit scared that they were going to hurt...nothing happened.

He broke away from me like I was toxic, I stared at him, he looked angry. Why was he mad? I knew I did nothing wrong.

"Are you okay?" I asked.

"Yeah." He closed his eyes for a moment. I heard him taking deep breaths.

"Are you sure you're okay?" I asked. He didn't look okay to me.

"I'm fine!!" He half-shouted at me. I stared at him with my eyebrows raised.

"You did not have to shout at me," I told him. "I just wanted to know if you were okay."

"I'm sorry."

"Whatever," I got up. I was leaving.

"Belle," Nate called. I met his gaze.

"I'll see you tomorrow," I told him and left.

~~~

That night, I took a nice, cold shower. I put on my bra and panty while I was still in the bathroom. I walked out of the bathroom into my bedroom and checked myself in the mirror. I caught a movement in the corner of my eye. I looked over and saw Nate watching me...I yelped.

I covered myself with a piece of clothing, ran over to the window, and drew the curtains closed. He could not see me anymore, I sighed heavily. I heard a soft chuckle__Nate was amused.

A few hours later, I had trouble sleeping, I decided to go to my window sill and gaze at the stars. Nate's bedroom was dark, he was probably sleeping or lying awake on his bed. I gazed at the stars for at least thirty minutes.

"Can't sleep?" A voice my soul would always recognize asked. I glanced at Nate.

"No."

"Me neither," He said. We stayed quiet for a moment, unsure of what to say to each other. "I'm sorry for yelling at you," He apologized.

"You don't have to apologize," I told him. I understood him. I mean, I could barely control my anger. I was worse than him.

"Yes, I do--" he said. "I'm sorry."

"You're apologizing a lot lately," I remarked.

A look of pain crossed his face. "I've hurt you a lot since you came back," he said and I could not disagree with him.

"Yes, you have." I smiled at him.

"You're supposed to say 'It's fine.'" Nate chuckled.

"It's fine," I said and we both laughed.

After we ceased from our laughter, I wanted to know something. "Did you cry when I left to Oregon?" I asked him.

Silence filled the air for a few seconds. "I was eight, a little boy with feelings for the girl next door--" Nate said. "Nothing's changed. Except now you have feelings for me."

"Did I really hurt you?"

"At that time, I blamed you, I felt betrayed by you." He told me. "I blamed you for not protesting to your dad."

"I did for a year," I told him and he smiled.

"As I grew older, I realized it wasn't your fault. Your dad hated me, he thought of me and still do as his enemy."

"I'm sorry."

"Every morning, I'd wake up and stare at the picture of us on my desk. I wanted to search you on Facebook, but I always thought there was no point." Nate told me. I was interested in knowing his version.

"I wanted to look you up too, but I got scared every time--" I told him.

"I remember the day you came back, I came into my room and saw you unpacking. Something about you felt familiar. You looked up at me and I felt like I knew you, but I wasn't sure." He told me. "The next day, you introduced yourself in English, my world had fallen upside down. The first thing I thought was how beautiful you've become."

"So, I wasn't beautiful back then?" I joked, smiling. He chuckled softly.

"We were young, I was still in the 'She's cute' phase." He laughed and I joined him. "I was rude to you, I didn't want to get attached to you again, but Tessa ruined your car, and the next thing I knew was, I was giving you rides and we were getting closer to each other."

"Until I got drunk and my dad blamed you--" I finished for him.

"I realized your dad would always be in your life and think of me as the enemy, so I pushed you away." Nate said. "But, you would not stay away, you climbed up to my room, and professed your feelings for me."

"I can never forget that day," I smiled. "You threw me across the room."

"You broke my bedroom door."

"You kissed me and told me you felt nothing." I reminded him. He looked away, embarrassed.

"I lied," he said quietly.

"Why?"

"I could not see us working out," he responded. "Protectors and Minders are natural enemies, Wolf-Shifters and Vampires are natural enemies too."

"I know."

"When you started dating an ordinary, I was so angry. I could not understand why you would risk yourself with an ordinary. Was he that special?"

"You were jealous?"

"Yes," he confirmed. "I was both angry and pissed when he cheated on you. I was pissed because you did not deserve a cheater, and happy because I figured you would dump him...you didn't. So I gave you roses as a reminder that___"

"You are the one my eyes glow for," I finished for him. "You followed me to the party, attacked him, told me to get into your car while glaring at me."

"I also kissed you," he added. I laughed softly, he had a smile on his face. A question came into my mind.

"You told me that your family thinks of Tessa as an abomination," I started. "Do they think of me like that too?" He stared at me.

"No."

"Not even Edward?" I asked and Nate chuckled.

"He's actually pretty fond of you," Nate said. I stared at him with etonnement.

"Really?"

"Yes...speaking of Edward, he wanted me to ask you to draw his future wife." I laughed. That was so Edward.

"Tell him I will do that somewhere in the future," I told Nate.

"I don't think he'll like that, he wants to know now." Nate told me.

"If he knows, it might affect his future." I said.

"I don't think so," Nate said. "Remember when you drew Tessa and I kissing on the porch and I said that Tessa and I were not going to happen, but we did. What if your power isn't seeing the future, but creating the future." I thought about what he said, that would have been pretty cool and scary.

"You read too many books," I laughed. "I'm a Seer, not God."

"I know," he chuckled.

We stayed quiet for a couple of minutes, gazing at the stars. With time, I became sleepy. I yawned loudly and looked at Nate. "I'm tired, I'm going to sleep." I told him.

"Sleep well," he wished me. I got into bed and slept well.

~~~

There was too much light, I didn't want to wake up, I was so tired. My bedroom door opened loudly, I quietly groaned. "Don't you have school today?" It was my mom, my eyes fluttered opened.

"Crap," I mumbled. I ran to my bathroom, brushed my teeth, washed my face, ran back into my bedroom, and started getting dressed.

"Aren't you going to take a shower?" My mom asked a stupid question. She was watching me putting clothes on, it was obvious that I wasn't to take a shower.

"No, mom. I'm going to be late."

"You're already late, go take a shower."

"First period has already started, I have to be in the class today."

"Why do you have to be in first period?" She asked suspiciously. Nate and I only had first period together besides lunch. I wanted to be as close to him as possible.

"Because English is not my first language and the SAT, ACT are coming up." I told her and ran downstairs. I ate cornflakes and milk real quick. I got into my car. When I tried to turn the engine, it would not start. At this point, I was frustrated with everything. I ran inside the house. "Mom," I yelled out her name. She appeared in front of me with her arms crossed. She could be so dramatic sometimes.

"Why are you yelling?" She demanded.

"I'm sorry," I apologized. "I need you to drive me to school."

"Why?"

"My car won't start."

My mom dropped me off, I was an hour late, I had twenty minutes left for English class. When I opened the door to English class, everyone got quiet. I quickly walked toward my seat and sat down. "Nice of you to join us, Rosabelle." The teacher welcomed me. Some kids snickered.

"Thank you." I mumbled under my breath. Nate was gazing at me. "What?"

"Did you take a shower?" He asked.

My blood boiled, I was embarrassed. "No, I overslept today." I told him. He nodded and looked straight ahead. Was my body scent bad?

"Do I stink?" I asked Nate. He gazed at me for a moment.

"You smell like a wet dog," he said and my eyes widened. A moment later, the realization hit him. He gazed at me, he looked lost. "You are able to shift anytime now," he said. I looked away, I was overthinking things. "Why aren't you excited?" I looked at him, unsure of what to say.

"I don't know."

"Are you nervous?"

"A bit," I said. "I'm a bit scared."

"Of what?"

"The pain," I responded. "I don't want to go through the pain again." It was half the truth, it was so much more than the pain, it was about everything.

"That can't be it."

"I don't like pain."

"No one does," Nate said. "It's a form of weakness." He gazed at me. His eyes were burning my soul. "What's really going on?" I shrugged my shoulders.

"I told you already, I'm not ready for the pain again." I told him.

"You're keeping something from me," he said. "Everyone has to deal with pain."

"I'm not 'everyone.' My bones will break when I transform, you have no idea how painful it will be." I said, looking at him.

"You will get through it."

"I don't think I can," I said. "I have 206 bones in my body. Last time I was on the verge of transforming, a few of my bones broke, the pain was too much for me that I passed out." I cringed at the memory.

"I'm sorry."

"If I could not stay awake that time, do you think I will make it through when I really transform?" I asked Nate. He looked honest.

"You are Rosabelle Foureau--" Nate began "--you can do it...if you believe in yourself."

"Do you believe in me?"

"Always," He responded and I smiled. He always knew what to say to give me the courage and confidence I needed.

"I need the two lovebirds in the back to pay attention to what I'm saying." The teacher said loudly, interrupting us. Everyone looked at Nate and I.

"Oh, we're not__" I hesitated and looked at Nate.

"We're not together," Nate said.

"I don't care if you two aren't together. I need you to pay attention." The teacher scolded us.

~~~

"Aren't you going to the library?" Samantha asked. I had just finished my lunch.

"What do you mean?"

"Ever since you and Nate got together, you always go to the library after you eat."

"I'm not going today."

"I'm glad because I have to tell you something about me and Dylan," she said. Dylan wasn't in school today.

"Where is he?"

"Boise," she said. "I wanted to tell you last night, but it was too late and this morning, you were late__" She had a look of excitement, it was contagious. "Last night, Dylan and I had a massive argument and we kissed." Samantha said. There was a moment of silence between us.

"WHAT!" I exclaimed. Both Samantha and I had huge smiles on our faces.

"I know."

"How was it?"

"Magical." She giggled. I've never heard Samantha giggling before.

"What was the argument about?"

"Supernaturals," she said.

I stared at her for a long time. How was that massive? "How is an argument about Supernaturals massive?" I asked.

"You should have heard what we said and called each other," she said.

"Was it bad?"

"No," Samantha said while looking away. Any small argument between Samantha and Dylan was massive.

"Were you two alone when you were kissing?" I asked and Samantha gave me a weird look.

"His dog was present."

"You should have called me."

"It was late, I assumed you were sleeping--" Samantha said. She looked sorry.

"I could not sleep last night."

"Me too," she said. "I stayed up all night thinking about the kiss."

"Have you spoken to Dylan today?" I asked her. She looked at me, her eyes were bright. What was wrong with her. I did not recognize her. She shook her head at me. "Why not?"

"He's spending the day in Boise and I don't want him to think of me as a clingy girlfriend if I call him--" Samantha said and I scoffed.

"You two were best friends before the kiss, he won't think of you like that." I assured her.

"He'll be back this afternoon. He's coming over to my house to study," Samantha said.

I looked at her, she looked back. A smile formed on my face. "'Study' huh," I mocked and winked. She cracked up laughing, I laughed with her. I knew it was not actually like that.

"It's nothing like that."

"Right," I mocked her.

"We study together all the time," She said. I knew that Dylan and her studied together.

"I believe you," I said and got up. "I'm going outside to breathe some fresh air, do you want to join me?"

"Sure."

We were walking halfway out of the cafeteria when someone pushed me into one of the trash cans. Everyone gasped and there was silence. Samantha quickly helped me out. "Thank you," I thanked her. I was so embarrassed, I wanted the ground to swallow me and save me from this embarrassment. I looked at the person who pushed me__it was Tessa. She had a smile on her face. I felt so much anger building inside me, I wanted nothing more than to attack her. I was trembling, my whole body was shaking. I could feel Samantha panicking silently beside me. She was glancing at Tessa, no doubt reading her mind. Tessa was still smiling. "Why did you do that?" I growled lowly at her.

"I was bored," she said--meeting my gaze.

"You were bored?" I scoffed.

"And annoyed," she added. "You always manage to piss me off."

"I stay far away from you as possible."

"But you don't stay away from him," she said. She was talking about Nate. I looked back at her in shock.

"Is this about him?"

"It's always going to be about him between you and me, Rosabelle." She laughed. "I know your little routine. Going to the library to be with him." She advanced me. "You sneaky, little bitch deserve what you will get." My brain started burning. I looked at Samantha, she knew what was going on. Samantha raised her fist and punched Samantha in the face. Again, everyone gasped. My brain stopped hurting, I was relieved.

"Come on," Samantha rushed me out of the cafeteria and led me into a bathroom. She checked inside the stalls. "No one's here," she assured me.

"What was Tessa doing?"

"She wanted to make you angry enough to transform."

"Why?" I asked. "That would have killed the ordinaries...why would she do that?"

"She is so angry about you and Nate that she wants you to feel pain," Samantha said and it all made sense. Tessa was so angry and jealous that she would do anything, even if that meant ordinaries dying to make me suffer.

If I had transformed in the cafeteria in front of the ordinaries, them knowing that my kind existed would have killed them and no ordinary doctor or scientist would have known their cause of death. Protectors would have had no choice but to punish me. "She wants the Protectors to punish me," I gasped.

"And remove your canines," Samantha added. This was bad. If my canines were ever to be removed by Protectors, there would be a war between Wolf-Shifters and Protectors. There would also be allies involved, that could only mean one thing.

"A Supernatural war," Samantha and I said in unison.

CHAPTER SIXTEEN

.

"She did what?" Nate asked. He was sitting on his window sill with Edward and I was sitting on mine.

"She needs to be put away," Edward said.

We all knew what that meant. "I don't think we need to go that far," I said. From what I could tell, The Protectors' punishment methods were harsh and no one should go through them.

"She tried to sabotage you. She was willing to kill ordinaries in the process," Edward said. Nate nodded at him, I shook my head at them.

"No," I firmly said.

"You have no say in this," Edward said.

"I'm the one she tried to sabotage," I told them. "I don't want her to be punished."

"She was willing to kill ordinaries," Nate said. I gazed at him in shock.

"Nate, are you serious?"

"I'm part Protector...my job is to protect ordinaries from Supernaturals like Tessa," Nate said.

"Are you hearing yourself?" I asked him. "We're talking about Tessa here."

"Yes, I am aware of that."

"She was your girlfriend for three years."

"That's how I know she won't stop until she gets what she wants, even if that means ordinaries dying in the process." Nate tried to reason with me.

"She does not deserve to be punished."

"What do you suggest we do?" Edward asked in a mocking tone. "Talk to her, ask her nicely not to do anything that might kill ordinaries?"

"Better that than punish her," I said.

"Why do you want to save her?" Nate asked. I stared at him for a moment.

"Why don't you want to save her?" I asked. I wanted to know the answer to that.

"She wants your canines to be removed...and you're trying to protect her." Nate rummaged through his mind.

"She's one of my kinds, I don't want her to suffer in the hands of people who are supposed to be my enemies--" I told him and Edward scoffed.

"Says the girl who's dating ONE of her 'supposed enemies,'" Edward mocked and looked at me. "The fact that she was willing to sabotage you, means that she doesn't care that you are also her kind. She doesn't care about you...you need to stop caring about her and let my kind and I do our thing."

"Nate." I looked at Nate, hoping he would say something.

"What?" He asked.

"Aren't you going to say something?" I asked. I really wanted him to agree with me.

"What do you want me to say?"

"I want you to back me up," I told him. I could tell that Edward was comfortable.

"Why would I do that?"

"She was your girlfriend for three years," I tried to reason with him.

"So?"

"Didn't you love her?" I asked. There was a moment of silence. Nate looked at me and met my gaze.

"I don't do 'Love,'" He said. It was like he stabbed me. I was in shock. Would he ever love me, I already loved him, I mean, how could someone be in a relationship and not love them?

I looked at Edward, he was speaking on the phone. "We have a Minder to handle," he said and hung up.

"What's going to happen to her?" I asked. I wasn't sure if I wanted to know.

"It's best if you don't know," Nate said.

~~~

"What are they going to do to her?" I asked Samantha and Dylan. We were in the cafeteria.

"I don't know and I don't want to know." Samantha said, "I want to have my innocence forever."

"Are you serious?"

"Whatever's going to happen to her, the bitch deserves it." She said and I scoffed at her.

"No, she doesn't."

"She used her power on me and you." Samantha said. "Getting your brain fried is not a sweet gesture."

"That's her specialty, she has to use it at some point--" I told Samantha.

"Does she?"

"You use yours all the time."

"My specialty does not give people pain." Samantha defended herself. That was a lie, if Samantha had not known about Tessa's first time, it would all have been different, everything that happened after that was based on that secret.

"It does in a way."

"Excuse me?" She asked in disbelief. I told her my opinions. She didn't like what I had to say. "It all goes back to you, you're with Nate."

"Your specialty hastened it, and now Tessa wants blood." I told her.

"And you think it's on me," she gasped.

"I didn't say that."

"You were thinking it--" she said, on the verge of tears.

I felt bad for a moment, but I was angry that she read my mind. I could never have my privacy with her around. "This is exactly what I'm talking about, my problems with you--" I started. Both Samantha and Dylan gazed at me. "--You're always breaking the walls of my privacy, this is exactly why I love hanging out with Tia and not you.

"Rosabelle," she whispered.

"I like Tia because when I say 'Guess What' she actually has to guess and not read my mind. I can tell her anything I want, but you just read my mind and know everything I don't want you to know--" I told her.

"Is this really how you think about me?" She asked. She now had tears in her eyes.

"Don't you know the answer to that question already?" I mocked her. "I need my privacy."

"Rosabelle__" Dylan warned.

"Shut up, Dylan." I shushed him. I turned my gaze to Samantha, she was crying. "Stay out of my head." I quickly got up and left. I knew I should not have put my anger on her, but I really wanted to be free to think whatever I wanted to think about. I was walking in a hallway when someone called out my name.

"Rosabelle!" Dylan called out my name. Samantha was with him, she was no longer crying. "Did you really have to say those things?"

"Yes."

"None of this is Samantha's fault, it's all on Tessa." Dylan said. "She's the crazy one, she always wants to get what she wants and when she doesn't, she goes crazy."

"I don't understand why you're defending her," Samantha said. "She wants the Protectors to punish you and remove your canines."

"I bit her."

"Because she was using her specialty on you," Samantha argued. She was right, I needed to stop defending Tessa, she was nothing but cruel.

"I always thought of Tessa as a bad person, but I never thought of her as a murderer." Dylan said quietly. We all stayed in silence for a moment, none of us wanted this to be real, having Tessa as a murderer and wanting to frame me. This was a lot to handle.

"People are not always what they seem," I whispered quietly. Tessa had surprised us.

~~~

I was in the forest waiting for Nate when I heard him approaching the near branches. I greeted him. "Hi," He greeted back. "Are you still mad at me?"

"No," I told him and he smiled. He placed a hand on my face, caressing my cheek.

"Good," he said and kissed me fully on the lips. I kissed him back, my body was reacting in a way I could not explain. I place a hand on his chest and the other one around his neck. I pulled him closer to me. He grabbed my legs, wrapped them around his waist. A moment later, my back hit the tree. I let out a small gasp.

"Careful, you're strong." I reminded him.

"Sorry." He apologized and kissed me again. We kissed for a while until we heard a sound, we both stopped. Nate put me down with gentleness.

"What was that?" I asked. Nate looked around, sniffing the air. After a moment, he looked back at me. By the look on his face, I already knew the answer to that question.

"Wolf-Shifters," he whispered. I started to panic, Nate and I had to stay a secret, I could not afford my dad knowing about us.

"Go," I whispered in an urgent tone. He stared at me for a second and was gone. I looked around the forest, thinking of what I should say to the Wolf-Shifters. I was also hoping that they didn't see or hear me and Nate. Because if they did, they would tell my dad and he would be furious.

"Oh," I heard a moan. 'What the heck?' I thought. I used my vision to see who it was.

I froze at the sight, it was Tia and a Wolf-Shifter--who was her boyfriend. They were making out on the ground__half-naked. "Oh, my Gosh." I gasped out.

As if Tia heard me, she gazed right at me. "Oh, My gosh!!" She exclaimed and pushed her boyfriend off her. They quickly put on their clothes--that were on the ground--and fixed their hair.

"Why bother?" I asked and approached them. Tia was blushing furiously. 'White people,' I thought. 'Always blushing.' Her boyfriend looked uncomfortable.

"What are you doing here?" Tia asked.

"I could ask you the same thing, but__" I stopped. I looked at her boyfriend and at her. I smiled. "I already know."

"Em, em." Tia cleared her throat and pointed at her boyfriend. "This is Louis."

I knew who he was already, but I was never properly introduced to him. "Hi," Louis greeted me. He was white, with blond hair and brown eyes, just like Tia, but she had dark hair.

"I'm Rosabelle."

"Leader," he bowed his head.

"I'm not one yet."

"But you will be," he said. I nodded, a bit unsure of myself.

"What were you doing here...besides the obvious?" I quickly added.

"We were checking up on the Wolves," Louis said.

"And then, we had a moment." Samantha finished. She gazed at Louis, he gazed back and their eyes glowed. It was one of the most beautiful things I have ever seen. I was speechless for a moment, I did not know what to say.

"Your eyes are glowing for each other," I told them.

"We know," Louis said.

"We are Essence," Tia said.

"What's that?"

"We belong together, it's like true love and soul mate__"

"But more," Louis added.

"You mean, you're each other's mate?" I asked.

They both scoffed at the same time. "That's for Wolves, Essence is for Wolf-Shifters." Tia confirmed. I had a question in my mind.

"Does Essence only work with Wolf-Shifters?" I asked. They both gazed at me with a questioning look. "My mom is a Minder, her eyes doesn't glow."

"They do," Tia said. "For a nanosecond, enough time for a Wolf-Shifter to see it."

"Okay," I said--looking away. "I have to go, feel free to go back on doing whatever you were doing." I walked away. When I stepped out of the forest, I saw Nate on his porch with Edward. I heard laughter inside his house, his whole family was here.

"Did you get in trouble?" Nate asked.

"No, it was Tia and her Essence making out." I said and Nate smiled.

"They were making out?" He asked and winked at me.

"Oh, my__" I started but was interrupted by Edward.

"What the heck?" Edward exclaimed, looking past me. I turned around and saw Tessa driving like a mad woman. She drove through my front yard, parked her car, and got out.

"Tessa, what do you think you're doing?" I asked her.

"I'm going to tell your parents the truth about you," Tessa said.

"What are you talking about?"

"I can't wait to see your father's face when he realizes how you are betraying him."

"What are you saying?"

"I've always known you were dumb." Tessa smiled at me. "So clueless."

"Excuse you?" I asked.

"I really don't see what you see in her--" she said, looking at Nate.

Nate approached her. "A lot of things I didn't see in you," he told her. 'Ouch,' I thought. Tessa looked hurt for a moment, but she quickly smiled.

"The things you say to make her feel good about herself," she mocked. "I think we know that I'm the real deal."

"You never were," Nate said.

"You still love me," Tessa said.

"No, I don't." Nate said. "I've never loved you." A sharp intake of breath was heard.

"We were together for three years, you must have felt something for me--" she pleaded.

"Yes, but not love--" Nate said. Tessa looked angry, she looked at me, her face held nothing but disgust.

"If I can't be with him, you certainly can't be with him." She said and started marching toward my house. "Mr. FOUREAU." She called for my dad. I quickly tackled her to the ground. Our bodies collided to the ground.

"Aaah!" I screamed in pain when my brain started to burn, my vision was getting blurry.

"You, bitch. I will make it my personal mission to make your life miserable--" Tessa said with so much menace.

"Back away from her now," someone commanded. It was Linda, some Protectors were behind her.

"Tessa William, you are under Tribulation." One of them said. Tessa looked speechless for a moment, I was no longer feeling pain.

"What?" Tessa exclaimed. Tribulation was another word for punishment, Tribulation sounded way worse than punishment__and it was. All Supernaturals were afraid of it, only Protectors used that word.

"For what?" Tessa asked in disbelief. There was fear in her eyes.

"Like you don't already know--" Nate said, shaking his head at her. Tessa gazed at all of us.

"I did nothing wrong," she said.

"You're under Tribulation for the attempt of murdering ordinaries," Nate said.

"What?" Tessa exclaimed. She looked at Nate and advanced him. Nate held his palms up, stopping her from approaching him further. He looked at the Protectors.

"Take her," he signaled.

"Nate," I gasped. Why would he do that, how could he do that? He stared at me, his face was blank.

"Nate, don't" Tessa pleaded. "I love you...I'm doing all of this because I love you."

Nate stared at her with a blank face. He glanced at the Protectors. "Now," he said and a Protector advanced Tessa. In a moment, the Protector fell on his knees, clutched his head, and groaned out in pain. Two other Protectors advanced her and both fell on their knees, clutching their heads.

"Now would be a good time to use your canines," Edward said behind me. I turned and glared at him.

"Edward, inject her now--" Linda commanded.

"My pleasure," Edward said and advanced Tessa. She didn't see him approaching her. He held the injection in his hand and with one swift motion, he injected whatever was inside it inside her neck. She looked at Edward in surprise, Edward had a smile on his face, no doubt enjoying putting down a Minder--especially Tessa, who had used her specialty on him before.

Tessa looked around, confused, I felt bad for her. Her eyes settled on me, her face masked pure hatred for me. I stood before her, looking at her with so much pity. "I will come back for you." she said with so much menace. "I will make it my life mission that you will be miserable for the rest of your life." I approached her, meeting her gaze.

"I would like to see you try," I told her. She scoffed at me with plain annoyance.

"I will," she vowed. A car came into view, it was my dad's. I now realized that he was not in the house. He parked his car, both he and my mom got out and gazed at the car that was on the lawn.

"What's going on?" My dad asked.

"Tribulation," Linda answered.

"On my property," my mom glared at Linda.

"This involves your daughter," Linda said. Silence filled the air. My mom and dad gazed at me.

"No," my mom gasped. Her face was mixed with emotions. "Not my daughter."

"What did she do?" My dad asked.

"It's not like that, I did nothing wrong." I quickly said. My mom gazed at the Protectors.

"What are you doing on this property?" She asked them. The Protectors looked annoyed for a moment. My mom was glaring at them. She hated them.

"One of your kind is under Tribulation," one of the Protectors said with disgust.

"Who?" My mom asked, looking at Tessa. She was making sure it wasn't me.

"It better not be my daughter...I think we all know the consequences of that." My dad said with a hint of warning. We all gazed at my dad.

"It's Tessa," Nate confirmed.

"Why is she being under...Tribulation?" My mom asked, not that much concerned, she didn't like Tessa for what she had done to me when I came back.

"For the attempt of murdering ordinaries," Nate told them. My parents were confused. "She tried to make your daughter angry enough to transform."

"In front of ordinaries," Edward added. My mom gaped at Tessa in disbelief.

"We need to take her away now," Linda said. They started to move Tessa, she still looked confused and lost. What was in that injection? I wondered.

"Wait," I called. "What did you inject her with?"

"Venom," Nate responded.

"What kind of venom?" I asked. I already knew, but I wanted to make sure.

"Wolf-Shifter," Nate responded.

CHAPTER SEVENTEEN

"No," I gasped out and met his gaze.

"Rosabelle, they've been doing this for a long time." My mom explained.

"Why do you think they remove canines?" My dad asked. I looked back at Nate.

"Tell me it's not true," I pleaded.

"I can't," he said.

I nodded my head, looked at the Protectors. I felt so many emotions building inside of me: sadness, pity, anger, and hate. "You all disgust me," I spat at them. The last thing I saw before I went back to my house was Nate looking hurt.

I slammed the door to my bedroom shut, I jumped on my bed and laid on my back. I could not believe Nate. How could he do that? Why would he do that? My bedroom door opened and my mom walked in. "Are you okay?" She asked and I mentally rolled my eyes. I really hated when people asked stupid questions.

"Do I look okay to you?" I asked her.

"Sorry," she apologized. "You are really upset."

"Of course I am."

"At Nate," she silently added. I gazed at her, she was observing me.

"What are you saying?"

"Is there something you want to tell me?" She asked. My heart was pacing.

"No," I told her.

"Are you sure?"

"Yes."

"You know you can tell me anything." My mom assured me. I looked away, unsure if I should tell her the truth or lie to her face.

"There's nothing to tell," I lied.

"Okay, I believe you." My mom said, making me feel even more guilty than I already felt. My mom got up and started walking away, but stopped. "I'm ordering pizza, what do you want?" I did not need to think about it.

"Pepperoni."

~~~

"I can't believe she's under Tribulation," Dylan said.

"Don't say that word, it's 'punishment.'" Samantha scolded at him. "Besides, I can believe it."

"What are they going to do to her?" I asked Dylan. He was a Seeker, he should know everything.

"They are going to keep injecting her with venom every day while she's under Tribulation...punishment."He quickly corrected himself for Samantha.

"How long will that be?" I asked.

"Thirty-one days," Dylan responded. "If a Minder is injected with Wolf-Shifters' venom for one day. His or her specialty won't work for a week. Can you imagine thirty-one days of being injected?"

"Her specialty won't work for thirty-one weeks." I said.

"This is perfect." Samantha laughed. "I can have seven months to be mean to her, annoy her, and piss her off without worrying about my brain burning." My mind was far away--thinking about Nate and his reaction to Tessa. "What's on your mind?" Samantha interrupted my thoughts.

"Don't you know already?" I gazed at her.

"You told me to stop reading your mind, remember?" She reminded me. "Besides, I actually can't read your mind."

"Why is that?" I looked at Dylan.

"Your whole body has venom now, even your tears. She can read glimpses of your thought, but not everything." Dylan said. Samantha looked impatient.

"Tell me?" She demanded.

"Nate was against Tessa," I said.

"Can you blame him?"

"They were together for three years," I said. "She told him that she loves him and__" I stopped talking for a moment.

"He what?" Dylan asked.

"He told her that he never loved her."

"Of course not, it's Tessa." Samantha said and I glared at her.

"He told me that he doesn't do 'love,'" I told them.

"Oh," Samantha said.

"How can I be with him?" I asked them, but myself in particular. Dylan scoffed at me.

"Now you're asking yourself that question?" He asked.

"Yes," I shouted at them. "I love him."

"Does he know that?"

"Of course not...and he'll never know," I told them. I could never tell Nate I loved him.

"You have to tell him," Samantha told me.

"To hear him say he doesn't love me back?" I asked.

"He might surprise you."

"Like he did with Tessa," I said. I saw Nate's car coming to the parking lot. "I have to go to my locker."

I went to my locker, placed what I did not need inside and took out what I needed. When I slammed my locker shut, I saw Nate. "Can we talk?" He asked.

"I have class," I told him and walked toward class. He followed me.

In English, we were discussing 'Things Fall Apart' by Chinua Achebe. The teacher was currently talking. Nate took hold of my hand, caressed it. I quickly looked around, no one was paying attention to us. "Talk to me," he whispered.

"I want to hear what the teacher has to say," I told him.

He kept stroking my hand and I was not complaining. I stared at the empty seat next to him. "Don't," he warned. I stared at him, he stared back. I detached my hand from his and got up.

"Mr. David, I'm not feeling well, can I be excused?" I asked. He simply stared at me, everyone was looking at us.

"Say 'please.'" I heard Samantha whispered.

"Please."

"Yes, you may." He said.

"Thank you." I thanked Samantha. I grabbed my things and quickly left.

~~~

I was outside in my backyard, laying down on the grass when Nate appeared. I quickly got up and watched him walking toward me. "What are you doing here?" I asked him.

"I came here to talk to you."

"My dad__"

"Just left," he finished. I gazed at him, he looked at me carefully. "Are we okay?"

"I don't know," I said and it was the truth.

"Are you still mad at me?"

"Yes," I told him. "I'm really mad at you."

"Why, is it about Tessa?" He asked as if he did not know already. I scoffed at him.

"It all started with her," I told him.

Something else was bothering me, I needed to tell him. "You're angry at something else--" he observed "--tell me."

"I don't feel like talking," I told him.

"The key to a relationship is to talk to one another," he told me.

"And you did not talk to me."

"What are you talking about?" He was confused.

"I told you that I didn't want Tessa to be punished, but you did not care."

"She deserves to be punished," Nate said. "She wanted to kill ordinaries."

"My transformation would have killed the ordinaries, not her--" I said to him. I gazed at him, he was glaring at me. I needed to ask him a question. "Have you ever injected a Minder with a Wolf-Shifter's venom?"

"Yes," he answered, looking away.

"Will you ever do that to me?" I asked him. He looked at me.

"Your whole body is filled with venom and your specialty still works...injecting you with venom would be pointless--" he told me. It was the truth.

"Will you ever remove my canines?" I asked him. He gaped at me.

"No." He gasped. "I will never."

"Have you ever done that to Wolf-Shifters?" I asked him. He was lost for words. "Nate."

"Do you really want to know?" He asked.

My breath was stuck in my throat. "Yes," he said. "I've done that."

"No--" I breathed out, stepping away from him. "Everyone was telling me the truth...they were all right."

"What are you talking about?" He asked, obviously confused. I gazed at him.

"You're a monster."

"I'm not a monster," he whispered. He looked hurt, really hurt that I would say that to him.

"Yes, you are. Removing a Wolf-Shifters' canines is so...inhuman."

"Is this how you think of me?" He asked me. "It was part of my training to become a Protector...I have to do inhuman things to Supernaturals that are endangering humans." He started to leave.

"Why would you do that to her?" I asked him. He stopped and looked at me.

"I did not have a choice."

"Yes, you did."

"I DID NOT!" He shouted at me. Surprisingly, I did not flinch. "She wanted to make you angry enough to transform and if you did, the Protectors would have blamed you because you could not control your anger...she was not going to stop until the Protectors had a reason to punish you."

"You still had a choice," I said.

"And I chose you," he told me. I gazed at him, his eyes were blazing blue today. My breath was caught in my throat. I walked toward him, pulled him close to me, and kissed him fully on the lips. He wrapped his arms around me and kissed me back. I tugged on his hair and bit his lower lip gently. He pulled me closer to him and kissed me deeply, it was getting hard to breathe. He placed one of his hands inside my shirt and stroked my back, I was playing with his earlobe while still kissing him.

He stopped kissing me on the lips and kissed my forehead in such a loving way. I felt so much comfort with him, he made me feel like I was everything to him. I placed a hand on his cheek. "I don't think of you as a monster, nor will I ever--" I told him. "I was angry."

"I would have been angry too." He half-smiled. He took hold of my hand that was on his cheek and kissed my palm. I grabbed hold of his chin and kissed him on the lips again. We kissed for a while until I broke away. He traced my lower lip with his fingers and I giggled. "Why are you giggling?"

"It tickles--" I told him, smiling. He smiled back and traced my lower lip again. I giggled harder. "Stop it."

"I can't," he told me. "I love the feeling of your lips underneath my touch." We stood there, gazing into each other's eyes.

"Nate--" someone interrupted our gaze, it was his mom. I stared at Nate.

"I have to go," he told me. I didn't want him to leave.

"Stay."

"I can't." He kissed me softly on the lips and broke away. I was still trying to kiss him, he chuckled and kissed me again.

"That was our first fight as a couple," I said after we broke away. He shook his head at me.

"Our first fight as a couple was over a Backgammon game," he told me.

"You remember."

"I thought I was never going to see you again, so I kept my memories of you intact."

"Nate, we have to go." His mom called out again.

"Duties call," he said and jumped effortlessly over the fence. I gazed at the fence for a few seconds before I walked back inside my house. I had a smile on my face. I was really happy, my heart beat for him, yearned for him. I loved him more than I did yesterday and my love for him was only growing more. It scared me, but it made me feel alive at the same time.

I was walking toward my bedroom when my mom appeared in front of me. She looked hurt. My smile faded. Was she okay? What happened? "Mom, are you okay, what's wrong?" I asked her.

"Why didn't you tell me?" She asked.

"Tell you what?" I asked with confusion.

"That you and Nate are together."

CHAPTER EIGHTEEN

"What?" I asked. My whole body was shaking, this could not be happening.

"I saw you two kissing," my mom said and I closed my eyes. A moment later, I opened them and gazed at her.

"I wanted to tell you."

"And you did not," she said. "I asked you so may times if something was going on between you and him...you kept denying it, you lied to me."

"I didn't want you to tell dad." I ran my hands through my hair. I was frustrated.

"I am going to tell him," she told me.

"That's exactly why I didn't tell you in the first place," I told her.

"Your dad has to know," she told me.

"Please, mom, I am begging you." I pleaded. My eyes searched hers. "Don't tell dad."

"Why should not I?" She asked.

"He'll do everything he can to keep me away from Nate...and I love him, mom." I told her.

"Rosabelle__"

"My heart yearns for him," I told her. She gazed at me, unsure of what to do.

"Your dad will be disappointed."

"I know."

"And mad."

"I know." She looked at me with a questioning look.

"You do realize that there is no future for the two of you, right?" She reminded me. I did not care about the future, I only cared about the present.

"Right now, I am happy. I'll worry about the future when it comes."

"I just don't see why you're risking yourself for him." She said, looking at me.

"You risked yourself to be with dad."

"Your dad and I are not natural enemies," my mom said. We said nothing for a few moments.

"Are you going to tell dad about Nate and I?" I asked her, praying she would not.

"No."

"Thank you."

"You will tell him yourself," My mom told me.

I gazed at her in shock. "You know I can't."

"Yes, you can."

"I don't want to."

"If you don't tell him, I will." She warned. I blinked at her, her face was serious.

"Mom, are you serious?" I asked in disbelief. She always had to tell dad everything.

"You know I don't keep things from your dad." She reminded me and I scoffed.

"You should start for the sake of your daughter," I said.

She stared at me for a long time. "You have until Friday to tell your dad," she said. I looked at her in disbelief.

"That's in two days!" I exclaimed. "I need more time."

"You've had time," my mom said.

"This is exactly why I didn't tell you about me and Nate," I told her and walked away.

~~~

"My mom knows about us," I told Nate.

We were inside his house, sitting on the couch in his living room. "I thought you weren't going to tell her about us," Nate said.

"Like your mom, she saw us kissing." I told him.

"Did she tell your dad?" He asked, concerned.

"She wants me to tell him by tomorrow."

"And if you don't."

"She'll tell him," I told him and he sighed.

"I think I need to start packing." Nate said and I laughed out loud.

"Nate, this is a serious matter." I hit him playfully.

"And yet, you're laughing." He smiled heartily at me. I gazed into his gray eyes. I was drawn to them, they were so beautiful. Without much thought, I quickly pecked him on the lips, he kissed me back before I had the chance to break away.

He pushed me down on the couch and climbed on top of me, still kissing me. I ran my hands through his hair and tugged gently. He let out a soft groan. I ran my hands down his back and traced his spinal cord. We heard the door opened. "Whoah, whoa, whoa--" Someone shouted. We both glared at Edward. "Is this what you kids do when adults are not around?" He mocked.

"Shut up," I demanded. Nate looked at me.

"Let's go to my room," he said. I wanted to, but I could not.

"I have to go home--" I told him, getting up from the couch. Nate followed me to the front door.

"If you want, I can be with you tomorrow when you tell your dad about us." I stared at him like he was crazy, he probably was.

"Are you out of your mind?" I questioned him.

"Maybe I am." He smiled at me. I placed a hand on his cheek and caressed him.

"I love your smile," I told him. His smile widened.

"I love the sounds of your laughs and giggles," he told me and began to trace my lower lip, knowing it tickled. I softly bit his fingers, he quickly pulled it out.

"Ow." He feigned being hurt. "I forgot that Wolf-Shifters love to bite."

"Especially things that are delicious," I added and winked at him.

He chuckled and pulled me toward him. "'Delicious' huh." He said--amused--and kissed me gently on the lips. I kissed him back with the same gentleness, he traced my neck in a delicious way with his fingers. A moment later, he broke away, the tip of our noses was touching. "Let's go to my room."

"And do what?" I asked. He stared at me.

"You know."

"I am not risking Edward walking in on us--" I told him quietly, looking around. "Besides, I want my first time to be special, your bedroom is not."

"What are you talking about?" He asked, confused. I stared at him.

"What are you talking about?" I asked him.

"I want us to go upstairs to my bedroom and do normal things--" he told me.

"Oh." I said, now embarrassed of my assumptions. Nate gazed at me.

"You thought I was talking about sex," he said and I looked down in embarrassment.

"Yes," I told him and he chuckled. My phone vibrated with a text message. It was from my mom, telling me dinner was ready. "I have to go," I told Nate.

"I'll see you tomorrow," he said. I nodded and left. When I opened the front door of my house, I met my dad.

"Hey, where were you?"

"Out--" I responded, looking at my mom.

"Where?" He asked.

"Lucien, you know the rules--" My mom reminded him "--no talking when dinner is on the table."

"Since when?" My dad asked, looking at her. Dinner was the only time we truly communicated with each other. My mom quickly glanced at me.

"Let's eat, I'm hungry--" I announced.

For dinner, we had spaghetti--my favorite food. We all stayed quiet, not saying a word to each other. The silence was really uncomfortable and odd. My dad kept clearing his throat over and over. "Are you__"

"Shh," my dad interrupted whatever my mom was about to say. "No talking when dinner is on the table, remember?" My dad was mocking her, my mom gazed at him with amusement. I was smiling at the two of them, they were a good example for me.

"I'm ratifying this rule," my mom said. It was my dad's turn to be amused.

"Why is that?" He asked.

"The silence is killing me," my mom told him and he nodded his head knowingly.

"How was your day?" My dad asked.

My mom let out a loud groan. "Terrible, don't even ask me about it--" she told him. She always said the same thing.

"Was it worse than yesterday?" My dad asked anyway. He always asked that question.

"Yes."

"What about you, Rose...how as your day?" My dad turned the question to me.

"It was good," I told him.

"I hope your day will be better tomorrow," my mom said and I gazed at her. Tomorrow was going to be the day that I would tell my dad about Nate and I being together. It could only get worse.

"I hope so too," I said.

Later that night, I was on my window sill, talking to Nate. He was sitting on his window sill. "Are you nervous for tomorrow?" He asked me.

"Yes."

"Me too," he admitted.

"I don't think it's a good idea for you to be here when I tell my dad about you," I told him.

"Why not?"

"I don't want something to happen to you," I told him.

He gazed at me. "I can take care of myself," He told me--trying to assure me, but I was not.

"I can deal with him by myself--" I told him, meeting his eyes.

"No, we'll tell him together."

"Nate__"

"We're in this together--" he said firmly, closing the discussion.

"Okay," I said.

~~~

"He's going to get his head ripped off," Dylan said. We were in the cafeteria, eating mashed potato.

"Why are you allowing him to do that?" Samantha asked me.

"Are you out of your mind?" Dylan asked.

I felt like they were targeting me. "I don't want him to join me when I tell my dad, but he wants to." I told them.

"Do you want to lose your boyfriend?" Samantha asked.

"Of course not," I said.

"You should refuse, tell him you want to tell your dad alone--" Samantha advised.

"Dylan, what do you think?" I asked Dylan.

Samantha and Dylan gazed at each other for a moment. "Base on your situation, this should be a father-daughter talk."

"Not a father-daughter-and-boyfriend talk," Samantha quietly added.

"Okay, fine."

I got up and walked to the library. I found Nate behind his usual bookshelf, I sat across from him. "What's going on?" He asked.

"I don't think it's a good idea for you to be with me when my dad learns about us."

"We already talked about this and agreed that we were in this together."

"I know."

"What changed your mind?" He asked.

"Dylan and Samantha."

"Oh, Dylan and Samantha."

"Yes," I said. "They don't think it's a good idea."

"I was not aware that Dylan and Samantha were in this relationship," he said.

"They were just giving their opinions," I told Nate. He gazed at me.

"I don't want their opinions."

"You don't, but I do...they're my friends." I told Nate.

"I don't want them to know about us, mingle into our relationship."

"They__"

"I told you once that I wanted us to be private," He reminded me.

"We are."

"No, we're not. You tell them everything that happens between us," Nate said.

"Like you don't tell Edward everything." I scoffed at him.

"I don't, he just finds out--" Nate said angrily.

I stared at him for a moment. "They are my friends, I can tell them things." I told Nate. He took hold of my hands and gazed at me.

"You can tell them whatever you want, but not about us." He told me.

"Why not?"

"I don't want them to know what we do," he said. I was confused for a moment.

"We don't do anything," I said.

"Not yet." He smiled knowingly at me. "This relationship is between me and you only. It's not between you, me...and them." I understood perfectly what he was saying and I had to agree with him.

"Okay," I said. He looked at the time on his phone.

"The bell is about to ring, do you want to ditch the rest of the day?" He asked.

"Where are we going?"

"Somewhere," he shrugged.

"What are we going to do?" I asked. He gazed at me.

"Do you have to ask?" He smiled. I smiled back at him.

"Meet me by your car in five minutes--" I said and left.

Five minutes later, I was standing by his car, watching him approached me. I laughed. He pushed me against his car and attacked my lips with kisses. I immediately kissed him back. I circled my arms around his neck, pulling him closer to me. The kiss was filled with hunger, we were savoring each other's mouth and I was out of breath. He stopped kissing me on the lips and moved to my neck. He grazed my neck with his fangs, making me feel pleasure. "Nate," I moaned his name. I opened my eyes for a second and saw my surrounding. My body was in a panic mode. "Nate, we're still in school." He broke away from me.

"Your dad's going to know about us," he said and kissed me on the lips one more time.

I kissed him back, but quickly broke away. "I want to tell him first...I don't want him to know about us by a Wolf-Shifter," I told him. Nate reached beside me and opened the passenger door for me. "Thank you." I smiled at him and got in.

~~~

I just took a shower, I put on my underwear and bra, wrapped myself in my pink bathrobe before walking out of the bathroom. I yelped when I saw Nate laying on my bed. "What are you doing here?" I asked him.

"Your dad, remember." He said.

"You can't just come out of my bedroom and tell him." I scolded Nate. "You need to go before he comes back." He was gazing at my bathrobe. "You need to leave."

"Why?"

"I need to put clothes on," I said. I stood in front of my mirror and fixed my hair.

"You have underwear on," He said and I froze. How in the world did he know that?

"How do you know?" I asked. A moment later, he came behind me, he was really close to me. He tugged at my bathrobe and my bra was showing. He took the bathrobe off of me, we gazed at each other in the mirror. He started kissing me on the neck, up to my ear. He quickly turned me around and kissed me on the lips. He picked me up and threw me on the bed. He climbed on top of me and kissed me again. I kissed him back, his hands were everywhere. His hands were now on my back, he took my bra off, my hands were under his shirt--tracing his muscles. He broke away and took off his shirt.

Oh, my.

I gazed at him, he gazed back, his hands were clutching my panties. He ripped the piece of fabric apart. I quickly pressed my thighs together and covered my breasts with my hands. He had this look of wonder in his face that told me to not hide, I relaxed myself. "Don't," Nate said--removing my hands from my breast and opening my legs wide for him. He gazed at me before he kissed me.

His hands and fingers were doing things to me that I could not imagine, I was experiencing so much pleasure, was that even possible? I questioned myself.

He stopped kissing me on the lips, he was moving south. My back arched when I felt his lips on me, my hands were tangled in his hair, his hands were squeezing my breasts. In that moment, I understood what he was saying in the library-- "I don't want them to know what we do." He meant this. "Nate," I moaned out his name. His eyes fluttered open and met my eyes, his lips were still doing wonders to me. He bit me gently, making me gasp.

My bedroom door opened, Nate quickly covered me with his body. My dad gaped at us in shock, my heart was racing. "What is this!!" He screamed at us.

"Dad."I started to panic.

"Get off my daughter," my dad glared at Nate.

"Sir, she's naked--" Nate stated. My dad was about to lose it, I felt his anger radiating from him.

"Dad, you need to leave so I can put clothes on." I told him and he scoffed at me in disgust.

"Now you want to wear clothes." He spat at me and left. Nate and I quickly got up and put our clothes on.

"I'm so sorry," He apologized.

"Don't apologize."

We left my room and walked downstairs, we saw my dad pacing the room back and forth, mumbling under his breath. When he heard our approach, he looked at Nate. "You better get out of here before I kill you," my dad warned. Nate hesitated, my dad started to advance him.

"Dad--" I warned, stepping in front of Nate.

"You," he breathed out. His face was full of disgust. "Opening your legs wide for him like a slut."

"Sir__"

"Shut up," he screamed at Nate and looked back at me. "Did you enjoy it?"

I said the first thing that came to my mind. "Yes." He slapped me and I fell on the ground. Nate was advancing me.

"Don't you dare step any closer toward my daughter." My dad snarled at him.

"Dad--" I pleaded, getting up

"Go to your room, Rosabelle." He looked at Nate, "Get out of my house." Nate started to leave when I reached for him. I was too slow because my dad grabbed my wrist, his claws dug into my flesh.

"Ahh!!" I screamed in pain.

"Stop, you're hurting her." Nate snarled at my dad, his fangs were visible. The door opened and my mom walked in.

"You won't believe what__" she stopped saying whatever she was about to say and gazed at us. Her eyes fell on my wrist, there was blood. "Lucien." My dad let go of my wrist. "What's going on here?"

"You had to be here," my dad told her. I looked up at Nate.

"I'm so sorry," he mouthed. All I wanted to do right now was to be in his arms. I was running toward him when I flew across the room and hit the ground.

"Lucien," my mom shouted angrily at my dad. "What is wrong with you?" Nate helped me up and pulled me close to him. I cried on his chest, he was stroking my back, I could tell that my dad was glaring at the site of us. I looked up at my dad.

"You're just a toy to him, he'll play you and throw you away at the end--" my dad said.

"I care for your daughter," Nate defended himself and my dad scoffed.

"He only cares for you...and here you are, falling deeper in love with him every day." My dad said and I froze. I could not believe that he said that in front of Nate.

"Lucien, that's enough." My mom said angrily. I could feel Nate's gaze on me.

"Is it true...do you love me?" He asked. I looked at my parents, I could not tell him because he didn't do 'love' and it would be an embarrassment in front of my parents.

"No, it's not true--" I said and my dad scoffed.

"Lucien, stop. You've hurt our daughter enough today," my mom said when my dad opened his mouth.

My dad looked at her in disbelief. "Our daughter was underneath him, fully naked." He pointed a finger at Nate. "With her legs wide open for him." My mom looked at him in shock, I saw disappointment on her face.

"Mom," I called for her. She stared at Nate.

"You need to leave," she said to him.

"Mom, it's not what you think--" I said and she ignored me.

"Got to your room," she commanded. I looked up at Nate, he didn't want to leave me.

"Go," I told him.

"Will you be okay?" He asked.

"She'll be fine," My mom told him. He looked at me, unsure. I smiled at him assuringly.

"I can take care of myself," I told him.

A few seconds later, after a few glares from my dad, Nate left. We all stared at each other in silence. I looked down at my wrist, I really needed to clean myself up. I started walking away when my mom stopped me.

"Where are you going?" She asked.

"I'm going to clean myself up." I said, not looking back at her.

I cleaned myself up, my wrist wasn't healed yet, and it would not heal for a long time. The fact that my dad and I were Wolf-Shifters and he hurt me, I would have to bear scars for a while. I gazed at myself in the mirror, my eyes were not swollen, but they were red from me crying by my dad's behavior and harsh words. "Opening your legs wide for him like a slut." "You're just a toy to him, he'll play you and throw you away at the end." The words were flashing back. I started crying again.

My dad and I had a very special relationship, we were close to each other, he always gave me flowers on Valentine's day secretly to make my classmates think that I attracted boys. I was his baby girl and I could not stand the fact that this could all change because of Nate.

Knock knock knock

There were several knocks on my bathroom door. I quickly washed my face and opened the door. It was my mom. She followed me to my bed and sat with me. "Rosabelle, we need to talk." She said.

"I'm listening."

"What happened between you and Nate__" she began, but I quickly interrupted her.

"We did not have sex," I told her.

"Your dad told me what you two were doing," my mom said. "I've never been so ashamed of you."

"Mom__"

"Rosabelle, I thought I raised you right."

"You did."

"I can not believe that you were doing this thing under this roof," she said.

"Mom__" I started.

"Rosabelle, I think you need to stop seeing Nate." My mom interrupted me. I gazed at her. I did not hear her right. "There's no future for the two of you."

"We have the present," I told her. She looked at me carefully, observing me.

"Are you okay?" She asked. I met her gaze.

"No."

"Your dad was angry, he did not mean any of the harsh things he said--" my mom told me.

I remembered dad looking at me with disgust. "He called me a slut," I told her.

"He did not mean it."

"Yes, he did--" I said "--you should have seen his face when he said those words to me."

"He loves you."

"Not anymore," I cried. My mom tried to comfort me. "Can I be alone?"

"Yes," my mom said and left. I pulled my blanket over me, turned off my reading light and cried once again. This whole thing should not be happening, my dad was supposed to be supportive no matter what. I was happy with Nate and that should matter to him.

I understood where my dad was coming from, Nate and I should not have done what we did under this roof, but he should not have said those harsh words to me and told Nate that I loved him, he had no right. I hoped that Nate believed me.

CHAPTER NINETEEN

For the rest of the week, I didn't have school, it was spring break. I stayed in my room most of the time, Nate and I never talked. He never came to his window sill when I called for him. I was warned that things could change between us.

My dad and I stayed far away from each other as possible. I always stayed in my room, I only got out of my room when he was not here, in his room, or dinner was ready.

Today was Thursday, I was currently eating cornflakes and milk when my dad appeared. He ignored me, pretended that I was not in the room, I did the same. He grabbed a glass of orange juice and left.

At dinner, we were in a silent mode, the mood was dark. My mom tried to lift up the mood by talking, we ignored her. My dad and I never looked at each other, there was a lot of tension between us. "Rosabelle, how's your spring break?" My mom asked. I looked at her. Did she even have to ask?

"Terrible."

"It doesn't have to be terrible," my mom said. "Do something fun, something that will make you happy." The only thing I wanted to do right now was to be with Nate, he made me happy.

"Nate--" I said, looking at her. I could feel my dad tensing at the mention of Nate. My mom noticed that too and gave him a warning look.

"What about Nate?" She asked. Her voice was soothing and encouraging.

"He makes me happy." I said.

We heard someone chuckled, we gazed at my dad. What was so funny? "That's never going to happen," he said. Both my mom and I stared at him.

"Dad."

"You and that filthy Vampire boy are over," he spat out in disgust. Nate was not filthy.

"He's not filthy," I said.

"I don't care," he said. "I don't want you seeing him anymore." I gazed at him.

"You can't do that," I told him.

"I just did," he said.

"Mom, say something." I looked at my mom frantically. She was the only one who could make my dad let me be with Nate and I needed her to say something.

"You need to listen to your dad," she said. I gazed at her in disbelief.

"No, mom. He's wrong." I told her.

"I'm doing what's best for you," he said. I met his eyes, I was really angry at the moment.

"What's best for me?" I questioned. "Do you mean what's best for you?" I rose up from my seat.

"Sit down," he warned. I quickly sat down. "I AM doing what's best for you."

"No, you're not!" I shouted at him. His eyes widened at me, I was taking this too far, he was my father and I needed to control myself. "Nate makes me happy and you don't care...You can't stand him."

"No, I can't stand him--" my dad confirmed what we all already knew. "I hate him."

"And I love him!!" I screamed at my dad. Both he and my mom gasped in shock by my behavior. I've never screamed at him before.

"Rosabelle, you need to calm down--" my mom suggested. I quickly glanced at her.

"Calm down?" I questioned. "He doesn't want me to be with Nate all because of hate."

"Rosabelle__"

"I love him, mom...my eyes glow for him."

The air was filled with silence for a couple of seconds. We all stared at each other, I could feel my dad's anger radiating toward me. My mom and him exchanged eye contacts. "Why did you deny it?" My dad asked.

"What?"

"Why did you deny your love for him?" My dad asked. My mom was curious. I could not tell them, my dad would laugh at me, and think of me as a joke. I gazed at him, remembering him telling Nate I loved him.

"You had no right to tell him," I said.

"Why did you deny it?" He asked.

"I didn't want him to find out by you," I said. "I want to be the first one to tell him."

"I don't think you should tell him--" my mom said.

I looked at her, "Why not?"

"I'm taking your father's side...I don't want you seeing him anymore." She said and I gasped.

"Do you always have to side with him?" I demanded my mom, I wanted her to take my side for once.

"Yes, I do...especially with what you two were doing under this roof days ago--" my mom said.

"For once, mom, I want you to take my side--" I pleaded her. She looked at my dad for a moment.

"I can't."

"You know he's wrong." My voice was pleading.

"We've made our decision...it's final--" she said and I gasped at her. I could not accept it.

"Mom, please."

"Rosabelle, you are forbidden to be with Nate--" my dad said. I looked at him. The word *'forbidden'* did not sound right. I hated his choice of word. I quickly got up.

"Where are you going?" My mom asked.

"I'm going to my room," I told her.

"You need to finish your dinner," my mom said in a commanding tone.

I grabbed dinner, I didn't want to finish eating with them, I was angry at them. "I'm going to eat in my room," I told her and got ready to leave. My dad quickly got up and pointed a finger at my empty seat. He glared at me.

"Sit down and finish your dinner--" he commanded. We stood glaring at each other, my mom said nothing. A moment later, I sat down and finished my dinner.

~~~

Today was Sunday, I was currently standing outside the church with my parents. Around me, people were talking, saying goodbyes. I saw Nate and his mom talking to each other. My parents noticed them too. "I find it interesting that he can step inside a church," my dad said. It was a bit interesting. As if he heard my dad, Nate looked up and met my gaze. He took a step forward and my dad automatically pulled me behind him. They exchanged eye contacts. "Let's go home," my dad said.

Moments after we arrived home, I saw Nate pulling up in his driveway. He and his mom got out. My parents were walking toward our front door but stopped when they realized I wasn't following them. "Rosabelle, come home--" my dad called. I looked at him and at Nate. Nate was standing on his driveway like he was waiting for me. My feet started moving, I was walking toward Nate with a smile on my face, he smiled back.

"Let her go," I heard my mom tell my dad. I reached for Nate just like he reached for me. Within seconds, our lips crashed together. Everything, the world around us disappeared. There were only us, Nate was my home. Both of his hands were on either side of my cheeks, my hands were on his chest.

He broke away and gazed into my eyes. I stared back into his gray eyes. I caressed him softly on the cheek. I quickly glanced around, his mom was smiling, my mom was looking at us in wonder. I didn't need to look at my dad to know that he was furious. "Are you okay?" Nate asked.

"I am now," I smiled at him and he quickly pecked me on the lips. I wanted more.

"I was worried."

"You were?"

"I felt guilty for putting you in this situation," he said. I stared at him, he did look guilty.

"Don't be," I told him.

He quickly glanced at my parents before looking back at me. "You need to go," he said and I nodded.

"I'll see you at school?" I asked, looking up at him.

"Our usual place," he said. I smiled at him and left him.

I avoided my dad's gaze and walked inside the house. I was walking upstairs when my dad stopped me. "Rosabelle, we need to talk--" he said. I looked at him.

"No, we don't."

"Watch how you speak to me, I am your father--" he warned me.

"Okay, father...let's talk." I said.

He gazed at me for a moment, calculating me. "What was that?" He asked me. He was asking about Nate and I kissing in front of him, especially when he hated Nate.

"That was us kissing."

"I know what that was," he said. "Why?"

"Because we have feelings for each other," I said. My dad looked furious for a moment.

"I thought I made myself clear...I don't want you and him together." He said.

"But I do, dad, this is my life." I told him.

"You're ruining your life by being with him," he said. I gazed at him.

"It's my life," I said.

~~~

On Monday, I went back to school. I was excited to see Nate. I went to my locker and saw Dylan and Samantha talking to each other. "Hey," I greeted them

"Hey," they greeted me back.

"How did it go?" Samantha asked. I looked at her, she could not read my mind like she used to, I really liked this Samantha.

"Terrible, he's forbidding me to see him." I told them.

"People still do that?" Dylan questioned.

"We are in the the twenty-first century," Samantha added. "Are you still seeing him?"

"Yes."

"Does your dad know you're going to keep seeing Nate?" Dylan asked.

Yesterday, I had told my dad it was my life. "Sort of...He's really against it." I told them and they both scoffed at me.

"Can you blame him?" Dylan asked. "Your dad and Nate are natural enemies...you're his only daughter, you're with the enemy."

"My dad needs to accept him," I said. "He needs to accept us."

Samantha was looking behind me. "Your lover is coming," she announced. I looked around and saw Nate coming my way. My heart started fluttering. Nate smiled, no doubt hearing my heart beating.

"Hi," Nate greeted me.

"Hey," I greeted back.

"We're going," Dylan announced and dragged Samantha with him--they were both smiling. Why were they smiling? Nate looked at me with a curious face

"Did you tell them anything?" He asked. I told Samantha and Dylan a lot of things.

"Like what?" I asked.

"What we were doing on Friday," he said. I quickly looked away, I was embarrassed.

"Of course not," I quickly said. "You want us to be private."

"Yes, I do." He said.

"Besides, I could never tell them." I told him and he raised his eyebrows at me.

"Why not?"

"It would not have been appropriate," I told him.

He observed me for a long time, I shifted from one foot to another. I was a bit uncomfortable. "Are you embarrassed for what happened?" He asked. I remembered my dad walking in on us and him telling my mom about it, I was still embarrassed.

"Kind of."

"Are you ashamed of what we did?" He asked, gazing intently at me. I remembered my mom saying she's never been so ashamed of me.

"A bit," I told him.

He took a step closer to me and grabbed my hand. What was he doing? We were in the hallway with people around us. "We don't have to do that again," he told me. I thought about it for a moment, about the pleasures.

"No, I liked it." I admitted and he smiled.

"Me too," he admitted and kissed me softly on the lips. I could hear people murmuring about us. He was kissing me in front of everyone, I kissed him back like no one was here, like no one was watching us having the time of our lives. After a few moments, we broke away. I gazed into his eyes.

"Why did you do that?" I asked him.

"Do what?"

"Kiss me."

"Because you're my girlfriend, I felt like it and I love the feeling of your lips against mine." He said, smiling.

"In public?" I asked.

"We only kept us a secret because your dad didn't know about us...he knows now, so why keep it a secret?" He asked. He was right about everything.

"You're right."

"Besides, I want everyone to know that you are mine and I am yours." He said. My heart picked up and he smiled.

"I really like the sound of that--" I said, looking down.

"But?"

"My dad doesn't want us to be together," I told Nate what he already knew.

"Of course, he doesn't." Nate scoffed.

"He forbid me to be with you," I told him and he shook his head in annoyance.

"When?"

"Last Thursday," I responded.

Nate looked at me for a moment with a smile on his face. I wondered why he was smiling, it did not make sense at all. "You kissed me yesterday...in front of your dad." He reminded me. I remembered perfectly.

"I know."

"And now you don't want to kiss me."

"I want to kiss you...but I don't want to do it in front of people." I told him.

"Why not?" He asked and I shrugged my shoulders. I had stage fright.

"I don't like public attention," I told him.

"Really?"

"Yes."

"Is that all?"

"I hate when people kiss in public, and I don't want to become a hypocrite by doing that."

"Okay." Nate smiled. "We'll do this at our usual place," He added and I smiled.

"You know it."

The rest of the morning was great, it was already time for lunch. I walked into the cafeteria, grabbed something to eat, I listened to Samantha and Dylan talk or flirt. I looked down at my watch, it was time for me to go to the library.

"Later guys." I said, getting up.

"Have fun with Nate," Samantha wished me well.

"Thank you," I thanked her and walked out of the cafeteria.

I was halfway to the library when I realized I was being followed. I stopped walking and glanced behind me. Two male Wolf-Shifters were staring at me. "Rosabelle," One greeted me.

"What's going on?" I asked.

"We are keeping an eye on you," One responded. His name was Tim, he was black with brown eyes just like the other one whose name was Allan.

"Why?" I demanded.

"Your dad ordered us to," he responded and I rolled my eyes. My dad really loved to order people around.

"I'm sure he did," I said. "Tell my dad that I don't want nor like people following me around...on his content."

"We__"

"I don't care," I interrupted Tim and started walking away, but Allan stepped in front of me.

"Where are you going?" He asked.

"Somewhere."

"Are you going to meet him," he spat at the last word.

"Yes, if you must know."

"Your father doesn't want you to go meet him," Allan said. My anger and annoyance flared up.

"I don't care if he wants or doesn't want me to go meet Nate--" I told Allan "--now, get out of my way." I advanced him with a scowl. He took a step toward me and stared into my eyes.

"No," He said. I quickly glanced around, it was just us three. I looked back at Allan and attacked him. Tim quickly tackled me to the ground, I tried to push him off me, but he was too strong for me, I had not transformed yet.

"Let her go," a demanding voice commanded. It was Nate, he was glaring at them.

"We don't take orders from you," Tim said.

"We are in a place full of ordinaries--" Nate began "--unless you want to deal with my kind...let her go." Tim let me go and advanced Nate.

"You can't do anything to us, you know what will happen--" Tim said. He was talking about Protectors removing canines.

"There are worse things to do to Wolf-Shifters than removing canines," Nate said. Tim and Allan glared at him.

"Let's go, Allan." Tim commanded. Allan stared down at me, he was quite intimidating. "Falling in love for a blood sucker...what good is it going to do to you?" He scoffed at me and followed Tim.

CHAPTER TWENTY

I knocked on Nate's front door, I heard people laughing inside of the house. Today was Thursday, Protectors liked to reunite on Thursdays sometimes. The door opened, I looked up at Linda. She smiled when she saw me. I smiled back at her. "Rosabelle, come in." She opened the door wider and I stepped inside. All of the Protectors glanced at me, they were quite intimidating, I quickly glanced at Linda.

"Is Nate here?" I asked her.

"He's in his room," she responded. I was immobile for a moment. I did not know if I should go to his room or just wait here. "You can go upstairs if you want." Linda granted me permission.

"Okay." I walked upstairs, aware of the Protectors watching me. I walked inside Nate's room. He quickly looked up and smiled. My body ignited for him.

"Belle," he greeted me and kissed my temple.

"Your kind was looking at me like I was the most interesting thing in the world," I told him.

"That's because you are."

"How?"

"You're part Minder and Wolf-Shifter...we're natural enemies both ways and here you are, in my room." He said and I scoffed at him. He smiled.

"Shut up."

"Do your parents even know you're here?" He asked. A moment later, he added-- "Does your dad even know you're here?" He was mocking me and I absolutely loved this side of him.

"Obviously not."

"Oh, I see." He placed a finger on his lips. "You're seeing me behind his back." He winked at me.

"Nate, stop." I hit him playfully.

"Ow," he feigned being hurt.

I laughed heartily at him. He looked at me with wonder in his eyes. He wrapped his arms around my waist and pulled me closer to him. "I love it when you laugh," he told me. I gazed at him, his eyes were smiling.

"That's because I'm happy," I told him and he kissed me fully on the lips. I kissed him back with so much passion, I placed my hands on his chest, I could feel his heart beating, I smiled. I broke away the kiss and pulled off his shirt. He took off my shirt, turned me around, undid my bra, and took it off.

He pushed me down on his bed, climbed on top of me, and kissed me again. I ran my hands up and down his spine. He shuddered under my touch. I giggled, still kissing him. He stopped kissing me and gazed at me. "What?" I asked.

"You're so beautiful," he said. My whole body, mind, and heart yearned for him. In that moment, I wanted to profess my love for him, he had to know.

"I__" He interrupted me by kissing me. I kissed him back and caressed his upper arms. He stopped kissing me on the lips and started moving south. He kissed my jaw, my neck, my shoulder. I was aghast, I was breathless.

He took one of my ladies into his mouth and played with the other one with his fingers, caressing it, making it harder. I ran my hands through his hair.

"Nate," the door opened. Just like last time, Nate quickly covered me with his body. We both looked up at his mom and Edward--who had a huge smile on his face. "Dinner's ready."

"What are you two doing?" Edward asked.

"Edward," Linda snapped at him and dragged him out.

Nate looked back at me. "Your mom was really calm, if it were my parents...woo." I did not need to finish this sentence.

"My mom likes you," Nate confirmed.

"My dad hates you," I told him.

"I know," Nate saddened.

I took hold of his face. "Just so you know, my mom secretly likes you--" I told him and it was the truth. My dad did not know that.

"How do you know?"

"I'm her daughter." I got out of his bed and put on my bra and shirt. I walked to his window sill and observed outside.

"What are you doing?" Nate asked.

"I'm jumping out--" I said, staring at him.

He stared back with confusion written on his face. "Why would you do that?" He asked a stupid question in my opinion. Wasn't it obvious?

"I don't think I can bare looking at your mom and Edward," I told him.

"Are you embarrassed?"

"They walked in on us doing...you know." I did not have the capacity to even say the words. Nate was smiling heartily at me. None of this was worth smiling.

"Your dad has walked in on us doing worse things," he reminded me.

"I know, I don't need to be reminded--" I told him. He nodded his head, still smiling.

"Shall we go?" He asked. I stared at him. "I want to walk my girlfriend out of my house properly and not have her jump out of my window like a crazy maniac," I laughed at what he said. He was funny today and I liked this side of him. I was so used to him being serious all the time, that his funny side was a bit odd...and charming.

"Okay," I said and he grabbed my hand. My whole body ignited just by his touch.

"Let's do the walk of shame together," he said and I laughed once again.

We walked downstairs, we heard people chattering, laughing, telling stories, having the time of their lives. I really loved this tradition...it was special. "Rosabelle, are you staying for dinner?" Linda asked. I quickly looked down, I could not look up at her, maybe for a week. I was embarrassed.

"No, thank you--" I quickly said.

"There's an extra seat."

"I'm fine."

"Are you sure?" She asked.

"Yes, I'm sure."

"You can eat in Nate's room if you want," Edward smiled and I rolled my eyes.

"Edward--" Nate warned, but Edward was not someone who would take warnings, nor was he ever.

"I'm sure there are other things you will do besides eating," he winked at us. I did not think it was possible to be more embarrassed than I already was.

"Edward Florus," a woman with dark hair and green eyes called--it was his mom. Edward looked at her with a huge smile on his face. This was not good.

"You will never believe what they were doing when me and aunt Linda walked in on them--" he started.

"Edward--" Nate, his mom, and Linda snapped at Edward. I was just standing here with my eyes closed, wishing the world to end his life at this moment.

"Calm down everybody." Edward tried to calm us down. "Clearly you don't want me to say anything."

"Duh," I mocked.

"Not that I can't blame you...it's embarrassing." Edward said. My eyeballs almost got stuck backward from rolling it too much. Edward was just too much.

"Are you done?" Nate asked him. Nate was clearly annoyed with Edward. I was.

"No," Edward said and we both groaned. "Can I give you two a piece of advice?"

"No," we both shut him down.

"I'll give it to you anyways," he said.

"Of course," Nate mumbled under his breath. I knew he was amused, he admired Edward like a brother.

"When you two are doing this kind of thing...please lock the door," he advised. Nate and I scoffed at him.

"How about you knock before entering," Nate suggested. Edward stared at him like he was crazy.

"Why would I do that?"

"Forget it," Nate said and pulled me toward his front door. He placed a hand on the back of my neck and kissed me. I wrapped my hands around his biceps, deepening the kiss. The kiss was sweet, gentle. I was aware we were being watched, but I did not care. I was lost in the moment.

"Kids these days are disrespectful, they just don't care about respecting grown-ups." We heard Edward scoffed. Nate and I broke away and glared at him. He quickly looked away. Nate and I looked at each other.

"I have to go," I told him.

"Can't you stay here for a couple of minutes?" He asked. I really wanted to, but I could not.

"My dad will wonder where I am," I told him and it was the truth. My dad was so suspicious nowadays.

"Let him wonder," Nate said. He was about to kiss me again in front of everyone.

"Not here," I stopped him. The last thing I wanted was another one of Edward's snarky comments.

"Let's go outside," Nate said. I stared at him like he was crazy, he probably was.

"Are you out of your mind?"

"What?"

"The last time my dad saw us like that...before last Sunday...he was furious." I reminded him.

"Last time I checked, you enjoyed it." He said, looking down where my private part was.

"Nate," I scolded him. He moved his gaze to my wrist, he held my wrist and observed the new scars I now had from my dad's claws.

"Why haven't they disappeared?"

"My dad is a Wolf-Shifter and I will be soon...it will take time." I explained to him. He kissed each one of my scars, my whole body felt fire for him. How could he make me feel this way. My whole body yearned for him.

"Nate."

"I'm so sorry."

"Don't be."

"He said terrible things to you--" he whispered lowly, only I could hear him.

"I know."

"He called you a slut." I closed my eyes--remembering that moment, my mom told me my dad did not mean it.

"Haitian parents tend to be harsh with words that they don't actually mean to say," I told Nate.

"I felt so much guilt over that," Nate said. I needed to lighten the mood that had just turned sour.

"Nate," I gasped and feigned sadness. "You actually have feelings." He laughed heartily at me.

"I'm not the monster people think I am," he said.

"And you'll never be," I told him. He pulled me to a corner where no one could see us or hear us and attacked my lips with his. The kiss was so full of hunger for a minute, our hands were everywhere, I broke away when I could not breathe.

I placed a hand on his chest and I could feel his heart beating, it was beating fast. Did I have the same effect on him as he had on me? I smiled at the thought of me having an effect on him. It warmed my heart. "Why are you smiling?" He asked.

"Your heart is beating really fast," I told him and he smiled. He had such a gorgeous smile.

"Only for you--" he said and I kissed him with everything I had. I wanted him to feel me, to feel my love for him, and I could feel him. I could feel his body coming alive under my kisses. When I touched him, I could feel electricities and sparks running through his veins and arteries...just for me. I knew he could feel me too. In that minute, we were the only two people in the world, the universe.

He picked me up, pushed my back against the wall and wrapped my legs around him while we were still kissing. Our kiss was full of hunger and something else I could not name. It was extraordinary and I was out of breath once again.

He stopped kissing me on the lips and moved to my neck. I took that time to catch my breath. He was laying kisses on my neck. A moment later, I felt his fangs on my neck. I desperately wanted him to bite me, but he would not. "What you make me feel," he said against my neck. In that moment, I knew it was time. I wanted to tell him, I needed to tell him. I could not keep this away from him anymore. It was killing me and he had to know.

"I love you," I breathed out. His whole body froze, he quickly let me go and took a step away from me. We gazed at each other, none of us said anything for a moment.

"What?"

"I love you," I repeated. My whole body was shaking with nervousness, waiting for what he had to say.

"Okay," he said. I stared at him in disbelief. This was not what I expected him to say.

"Okay?" I repeated. "Is that all you're going to say?"

"What do you want me to say?" He asked. I gazed at him in wonder, like he was a strange thing of this world.

"I want you to say something else."

"Thank you for your confession," he said.

He was unbelievable, I just could not believe him. I was really hurt at this point and he knew it. "I want you yo say something other than '*okay*' or '*thank you for your confession*.'" I told him. Nate was the first person besides my parents that I have said '*I love you*' to. "For God's sake, Nate. I just told you '*I love you*.'"

"I didn't tell you to."

"You did not have to," I told him. "I just felt the need to say it to you."

"Well, I don't feel the need to say it back." He stabbed me in the heart with his words. I was on the verge of crying, but I held in my tears. I did not want him to see me like this.

"Are you serious?"

"You can't tell me you love me and expect me to say it back--" he told me and he was right, but I could not accept that.

"Wow." I looked at him.

He ran his hand through his hair, he was clearly frustrated. "Look," he said. "I can't do this right now." That was the best thing he said so far after I had professed my love for him.

"I agree," I said and started to walk away.

"Where are you going?" He stopped me.

"I'm leaving."

"I told you once that I didn't do '*love*,'" he reminded me. I remembered that time when he told me, I was still hoping it was for Tessa and not me.

"My bad," I whispered and left.

~~~

I walked into English class with my head held high, ignoring Nate's gaze on me. I had nothing to say to him and I certainly did not want to hear anything he had to say, I have heard enough already.

"Good morning, class." The teacher greeted us. No one greeted him back, Samantha had a look of disgust on her face.

"He got lucky last night...and this morning," she said. I really did not need to know this.

"Shh," Nate shushed her. Samantha went quiet. After several minutes, we heard her gagging. Nate and I looked at her, she was doing horrible facial expressions. What was going on with her? What was happening?

"Samantha, are you okay?" I asked in a caring way.

Samantha looked at me, quickly glanced over at the teacher and gagged once again. 'What the heck?' I thought. "He's replaying last night and this morning in his head," Samantha told us. 'Poor teacher,' I thought. No one was safe with their thoughts when Samantha was around.

"Samantha, leave the poor teacher alone--" I told her. She quickly glanced at me.

"I'm so disgusted," she said.

"It is a disgusting thing when you think about it," I admitted. Nate quickly looked at me in disbelief. I ignored his gaze.

"I can see everything...EVERYTHING!" She half-yelled. Everyone looked at her.

"Samantha, shh." The teacher commanded. "You're interrupting my thoughts." Nate stifled a laugh.

"Disgusting thoughts," Samantha mumbled quietly to herself.

"Get out of his head," I scolded her. She looked at me with sincerity.

"I'm scarred for life," she told me.

"You deserve it," I said--looking away. "That's what you get for reading his private thoughts," I told her. "I'm sure the nurse can heal you." Samantha quickly got up after I said that. The teacher looked up at her.

"Mr. David, can I be excused?" The teacher stared at her. "Please," Samantha quickly added and I smiled.

"Where are you going?" The teacher asked.

"To the nurse."

"Why?" The teacher asked.

Everyone was looking at Samantha and the teacher back and forth. "You really don't want to know the answer to that question," Samantha told him and it was the truth. If he knew the answer to that question, he would die, and the Protectors would punish Samantha or put her under Tribulation, as they liked to call it.

"Then no, Samantha, you may not be excused." The teacher told her. Samantha was annoyed.

"Mr. David, you don't understand." She protested.

"Sit down, Samantha." He commanded. Everyone was watching her, I was praying to God that she would sit down, but Samantha being Samantha__

"But it is important."

"I'm sure it is," the teacher said in a sarcastic tone.

After a moment, Samantha sat down, she was pissed. About five seconds later, she got up. This could not be good. "I'm on my period and I need a tampon...do you have a tampon...do you have one?" She asked the teacher.

"No."

"My period cycle is important...it is about hormones...and blood." She finished. Nate was coughing repeatedly. Samantha had to drag the word '*blood*' in her false excuse. Everyone was looking at the teacher now.

"You may be excused, Samantha." He said. Samantha smiled in triumph. She grabbed her things and looked at me.

"The P-card...works every time with males," she said and left. I could not believe she had the courage to use the P-card as an excuse. I admired her a little for that.

"Em, em." Nate cleared his throat. I ignored him. "Rosabelle, we need to talk."

"I don't want to talk."

"We have to talk."

"No, we don't."

"Rosabelle, talk to me." He pleaded. "What's on your mind?" He wanted to know what was on my mind, he had it coming.

"I'm thinking that my dad might be right about you," I told him. He looked confused for a moment.

"What?"

"I'm just a toy to you that you play with."

"Rosabelle__"

"And yesterday you threw me away like I was trash," I told him and he looked hurt. That would have broken my heart, but he had already broke mine.

"That is not true," he said. I went back to ignoring him. "Rosabelle," he called my name.

"Leave me alone," I commanded and he did.

The day went fast, it was already time to leave, I could not wait to go home, I was hungry, and I needed to eat something. I was walking toward the exit when someone pulled me inside a dark room, I knew it was Nate. He switched on the lights, I looked at my surroundings. Memories came flashing back. "Oh, wow, the janitor's closet--" I said. I was unpleased. The last time I was in here, I had cried.

"Do you remember what you said the first time we were here?" Nate asked.

"I have a good memory."

"Can you say it again?"

"Why?" What was he planning?

"Just say it," he told me.

"Oh, wow, the janitor's closet...are we going to make out?" I asked him and he smiled, unlike last time.

"Yes, we are." He said and kissed me. I let myself go and kissed him back. He pulled me closer to him, crushing me against his body. The kiss was fast, full of hunger, and desires. Electricity, sparks, fire ignited through our bodies, uniting us as one. He slowly broke away and gazed at me. I gazed back.

"I feel love for you," he said.

"What?"

"Your dad was wrong...you're not a toy to me. I will never play you and throw you away at the end." He told me, still gazing at my chocolate-brown eyes with his gray eyes that looked blue today...and for a nanosecond, his eyes glowed. "I care for you...I feel love for you."

CHAPTER TWENTY-ONE

"What?" I asked him.

"Please don't make me say it again--" he pleaded, but I wanted to hear him say it again. I wanted to be sure of what I had just heard.

"Say it again."

"I feel love for you," he said and I smiled.

The last time we were in this janitor's closet, he had told me that he felt nothing for me--breaking my heart into shattered pieces, and now he was telling me that he felt love for me--picking the shattered pieces of my heart, healing it. "So you love me." I smiled at him.

"Saying 'I *love you*' is meaningless to me."

"Why?"

"People say it to get what they want and a lot of times they don't mean it--" he told me and I knew it was true.

"I meant it when I said it to you."

"I know, your eyes glowed so bright...the brightest I've ever seen them when you said it." He told me.

"They only glow for you," I told him.

"I know. If my eyes could glow, they would only glow for you, only you."

"I know," I said. There was a question on my mind. I needed to ask him about it. "You told me that you didn't do love."

"I've never felt love for Tessa or Lena...you are the only one--" he told me."--I've never felt love for anyone who isn't you."

Suddenly, a force drove through me, I grabbed him by the collar and kissed him with a force. He pushed me against something, things fell on the ground, neither of us cared. His lips were moving violently against mine. It was like he could not get enough of me.

I ran my hands through his dark hair, he ran his hands down my back--making me shudder, he smiled against my lips for a second. The kiss was amazing and I enjoyed every second of it.

The door opened, it was the janitor. He looked at the things that had fallen on the floor and gazed back at us. Nate and I quickly picked up the things that were on the floor. "Don't worry, we're leaving." Nate assured him and dragged me out of the closet. When we were out of the school's building, we laughed so hard and we kissed one more time.

~~~

I was in the family room, watching a movie with my parents when someone knocked on the front door, my dad stopped the movie while I walked toward the door, I opened it to reveal Linda, she smiled when she saw me. "Are your parents home?" She asked.

"Yes," I responded. Soon enough, my parents came behind me.

"What are you doing here?" My mom asked Linda.

"Since our kids are dating each other, I want us to have dinner...all of us." She told them.

"No," my mom and dad said at the same time.

"Please, mom. I want to see him more often, I only see him at school--" I pleaded. We heard Linda coughing. She knew it was a lie. My mom observed me for a moment.

"What time?" She asked Linda.

"7:30. My house tomorrow," Linda told us.

After a few moments, she left.

"I did not agree to do this," my dad told my mom.

"Majority rule, Lucien." My mom said. "Linda, Rosabelle, and I have agreed to have dinner together except for you." My mom explained to him.

"I don't want to sit at the same table with that bloodsucker," he expressed his opinions. Clearly, he was frustrated.

"Well, I don't want to sit with a Protector, but I will--" my mom told him. My dad gazed at me for a moment.

"Fine," he finally said.

~~~

Today was Saturday, my parents and I were standing outside of Nate's front door, neither of them was going to knock, it was like they were afraid of touching the door. With a heavy sigh, I knocked on the door. Moments later, Linda opened the door. "Come in," she welcomed us. We walked in the living room, there were only six seats at the table. I saw Nate and Edward. Edward was about to take a seat when Nate whispered something in his ear. Edward nodded and sat beside my parents--who were already in their seats.

There were only two available seats, Nate was standing behind a chair, signaling me to come over. After we all took our seats, we began to eat. We were all keeping a light conversation. No one was saying much except for Edward, who was talking to my mom--who was trying her hardest not to be disgusted by him. "There was this girl, you know her, you flew her mom a couple of feet with your specialty--" Edward began.

"Tessa," my mom said.

"Yes...his crazy ex." He nodded toward Nate.

"What about her?"

"She used her specialty on me during a Thanksgiving dinner," Edward told my mom. We were all watching him carefully.

"What did you do?"

~~~

I was in the family room, watching a movie with my parents when someone knocked on the front door, my dad stopped the movie while I walked toward the door, I opened it to reveal Linda, she smiled when she saw me. "Are your parents home?" She asked.

"Yes," I responded. Soon enough, my parents came behind me.

"What are you doing here?" My mom asked Linda.

"Since our kids are dating each other, I want us to have dinner...all of us." She told them.

"No," my mom and dad said at the same time.

"Please, mom. I want to see him more often, I only see him at school--" I pleaded. We heard Linda coughing. She knew it was a lie. My mom observed me for a moment.

"What time?" She asked Linda.

"7:30. My house tomorrow," Linda told us.

After a few moments, she left.

"I did not agree to do this," my dad told my mom.

"Majority rule, Lucien." My mom said. "Linda, Rosabelle, and I have agreed to have dinner together except for you." My mom explained to him.

"I don't want to sit at the same table with that bloodsucker," he expressed his opinions. Clearly, he was frustrated.

"Well, I don't want to sit with a Protector, but I will--" my mom told him. My dad gazed at me for a moment.

"Fine," he finally said.

~~~

Today was Saturday, my parents and I were standing outside of Nate's front door, neither of them was going to knock, it was like they were afraid of touching the door. With a heavy sigh, I knocked on the door. Moments later, Linda opened the door. "Come in," she welcomed us. We walked in the living room, there were only six seats at the table. I saw Nate and Edward. Edward was about to take a seat when Nate whispered something in his ear. Edward nodded and sat beside my parents--who were already in their seats.

There were only two available seats, Nate was standing behind a chair, signaling me to come over. After we all took our seats, we began to eat. We were all keeping a light conversation. No one was saying much except for Edward, who was talking to my mom--who was trying her hardest not to be disgusted by him. "There was this girl, you know her, you flew her mom a couple of feet with your specialty--" Edward began.

"Tessa," my mom said.

"Yes...his crazy ex." He nodded toward Nate.

"What about her?"

"She used her specialty on me during a Thanksgiving dinner," Edward told my mom. We were all watching him carefully.

"What did you do?"

"I threw the turkey at her face, knocked her out." He stared impassively at my mom when he said that.

"Edward," Linda snapped at him.

My mom stared at Edward with a small smile on her face. This was not good. "My specialty is water, I can make you drown." My mom told him with a clear warning. Edward cleared his throat.

"Mom," I scolded her. Nate whispered something in my ear and I laughed. I gazed at him, he was smiling. He took hold of my hand and softly kissed my knuckles...in front of them...in front of my dad. I quickly glanced at my parents, my mom was smiling, and my dad had a scowl on his face. I was not surprised. Nate cleared his throat.

"May we be excused, I would like to give Belle a tour." Nate asked.

"Yes," Linda said.

"No," my dad said. Everyone looked at my mom.

"Five minutes," she gave us.

My dad was about to protest when Edward rose up from his seat. "Don't worry, Papa Wolf. I'll make sure monster here--" he pointed at Nate "--don't do anything inappropriate to your daughter." All of us, except for my parents, glared at Edward.

Nate and I got up from our seats, he placed a hand on my back and guided me away. We went to a room that had an Xbox. I gazed at him in shock. "You play Xbox?" I asked.

"Edward," he nodded at Edward. "I like to read books."

"I noticed." I smiled at him. He looked at Edward.

"I want to be alone with Belle," Nate told him.

"Don't do anything inappropriate to her, I don't want Papa Wolf to rip your head off--" he said and left. I turned my back on Nate and gazed at the room. A moment later, he wrapped his arms around me and bit my left ear softly.

"Nate," I smiled. He turned me around.

"You look beautiful today."

"Am I not every day?" I mocked him.

"You're always beautiful," he said and kissed me. The kiss was filled with passion, hunger, desire, and love. "I feel love for you," he mumbled against my lips.

"I feel more love for you," I told him and he broke away.

He gazed at me, his gray eyes burned through mine. "Not possible," he whispered softly and I attacked his lips with mine. We kissed for a long time. Somehow, we made it to the couch, he was on top of me, I ran my hands through his hair. We were completely lost in each other.

"Em, em--" we heard Edward cleared his throat. Nate and I broke away and fixed ourselves. "Your parents are leaving."

Nate and I walked outside of the room, holding hands. My dad saw us, I wanted to detach my hand from Nate's, but he held on firmly. My dad glared at Nate for a moment.

Nate ignored him and kissed me softly on the lips. "Good night," he whispered...and his eyes glowed for a nanosecond. My heart fluttered.

"Good night," I told him. I looked at Linda-- "Thank you for dinner."

"You're welcome," she said. My parents and I left after that.

"I swear, he did that to piss me off--" my dad told my mom when we walked in our house.

"Well, it worked--" my mom told him.

Later that night, I woke up because I was thirsty and I needed water. I got out of bed, I heard my parents arguing, they rarely argued with each other, I focused on my hearing. "I don't see why you're supporting this relationship--" I heard my dad say.

"I saw the way he looked at her...she's happy," my mom told him and I smiled.

"She won't be for long."

"She is now and that's all that matters."

"Are you aware of the devastation she is going to be in after she transforms?" My dad asked her.

"Yes, I am."

"She's going to be sad and heartbroken."

"At least she's happy for now," my mom said. "We'll figure things out after she transforms."

"It will already be too late."

"It's already late, Lucien--" my mom told him "--Rosabelle already loves him and there's nothing we can do about it."

"Don't you think I know that?" My dad asked her. "If there was something that could be done, I would have done it already." It was the truth. My dad would have done anything to keep my heart from being broken if he could. He was very protective of me.

"I know you would, Lucien--" my mom said.

Silence filled the air for a couple of seconds. "His eyes glowed for a nanosecond, enough time for me to witness it--" my dad breathed out.

"What?" My mom gasped.

"I never wanted to believe it but now I am certain of it," my dad said.

What was he talking about? "You know what this means right?" My mom asked. 'What is going on?' I wondered. I hated not knowing anything, I hated being in the dark, I wanted to know everything.

"Yes."

"Are you sure about it?"

"Yes," my dad answered. "Rosabelle and Nate...they are Essence."

CHAPTER TWENTY-TWO

Today was Wednesday, I never asked anyone about Nate and I being Essence. I was currently helping my mom with dinner when I thought of Nate. "Hey, mom. Can I ask you something?" I asked--hoping she would be okay with what I was going to ask, I was sure she would.

"Anything."

"Can I invite Nate for dinner?"

"When?"

"Now."

"Now?" She repeated.

"Yes."

"Are you sure about this?" She asked, gazing at me. "Your dad won't like this and might say rude things."

"We've had dinner at his house twice, it's time for Nate to have dinner with us--" I told her.

"You're right," she said and I smiled.

"Can I go tell him?"

"He didn't know about this?" My mom asked.

"No, I just thought about it just now--" I told her.

"Be quick, dinner's almost ready."

"Thanks, mom." I thanked her and ran towards Nate's house. I knocked on the door, Linda answered. "Is Nate home?"

"He's in his room," Linda told me.

I stepped inside the house and looked at her. "Why are you okay with Nate and I being together?" I asked her. I really wanted to know the answer to that question.

"You make him happy, and seeing my son happy makes me happy--" she told me.

"He makes me happy too."

"He loves you," she said. "I don't know if he already told you, but he does." My heart melted.

"In a way," I told Linda. We smiled at each other for a moment.

"You can go to his room," she said.

"Thank you," I thanked her and went to his room.

"What's up?" Nate asked when I walked into his room.

"Have you had dinner already?" I asked him.

"No, why?"

"Can you come have dinner with me and my parents?"

"Now?"

"Yes."

"Is your dad okay with that?" He asked.

"My mom is."

"Your dad?"

"He doesn't know about it."

"Will he be okay with it?" He asked.

"He will have to be," I said. He thought about it for a moment.

"Okay, let's go." He said and I smiled.

Dinner was awkward, my dad was quiet. My mom kept the conversation going, thank God. Nate was comfortable with her, which was a good thing, they even shared a couple of jokes. "When did you two get together?" My mom asked. Nate and I smiled at the memory.

"Valentine's day...or should I say night." Nate smiled and held my free hand with his. My dad stared at our hands for a moment.

"You gave Rosabelle one hundred roses, that was so romantic...don't you think, Lucien?" My mom asked my dad. Nate and I gazed at him.

"You could say that," my dad said.

"Belle deserves more than one hundred roses," Nate said and tugged my ear. My mom had a huge smile on her face. My dad suddenly got up from his seat.

"Lucien, what are you doing?" My mom asked.

"I'm leaving."

"Why?"

"I can no longer look at my daughter with this bloodsucker--" he said and I got up from my seat.

"Nate hasn't sucked anyone's blood," I defended Nate.

"He will one day," my dad spat.

"You know what, dad, you can stay. Nate and I are leaving." Nate quickly got up from his seat.

"Where are you going?" My dad asked.

"My room."

"Over my dead body, he will not step a foot in your room." My dad said. For a black person, I could see his veins popping.

"Nate, let's go to your place."

"No, you're staying here."

"Mom?"

"You can go," my mom granted me permission.

My dad glared at Nate. "You can say you care about her, but you don't--" my dad said.

"I___" Nate began.

"If you ever did, you would stop seeing my daughter." My dad interrupted him. My mom gave my dad a cold look.

"Lucien, you have no right to say that--" my mom said.

"Do you know what's going to happen to her after she transforms?" My dad ignored my mom. "She's going to be heartbroken all the time, she will go to depression."

"I'M NOT TRANSFORMING!" I yelled. Everyone stared at me in shock. My dad looked like he got stabbed. "I want to be with Nate, my transformation will get in the way."

"You're making a big mistake," my dad warned.

"I'm not. Nate, let's go."

Nate and I left my house, we walked toward his porch and sat on the steps. "Is it true?" Nate asked. "Are you going to be heartbroken all the time?" I looked at him.

"I'm not transforming anymore."

"Transforming is a huge deal to Wolf-Shifters, it's a celebration. I don't want to be responsible for you deciding not to transform," Nate said. I held his hand with mine and stared into his eyes.

"You're not, it's my choice." I told him.

"Are you sure about this?"

"Yes." I smiled at him. In the distance, we heard my parents arguing. They were speaking Creole, only I could understand them.

"What are they saying?" Nate asked.

"It doesn't matter," I told him.

I focused my hearing on what my parents were saying. "The last time a Wolf-Shifter didn't want to transform, he died." I heard my dad say.

"That was just one," my mom said.

"Three Wolf-Shifters died because they would not transform," my dad told her. I wondered why.

"Why is that?"

"The first time a Wolf-Shifter transforms, the bones break little by little and it takes time. Rosabelle will transform eventually and her bones will break all at once...the pain will be unbearable, she won't survive." My dad told my mom and I froze.

"No," my mom breathed out.

"She will die," my dad said. "I will lose my baby girl."

~~~

Today was the sixth of July, it was night. I was currently at a party. It was fun, the music was loud, people were dancing around, more like grinding against each other. The party was in the forest, there were no ordinaries here. "Hey, Rosabelle." Samantha slurred behind me. Dylan laughed. They were really drunk. Samantha gave me her cup, I tasted the liquid that was inside of it and gave it back to her.

"Where's Nate?" Dylan asked.

"He's coming," I told him.

"Rosabelle, come dance with us." Samantha slurred. Dylan laughed harder.

"You two need to sober up, you're really drunk." I advised them while laughing. They looked hilarious.

"We'll do that," Dylan said and they left.

I stood alone for about ten minutes. Nate still hadn't shown up. I walked deeper into the forest for a while so I could think things through. My parents have been forcing me to transform, but I had not. I had to admit, I was scared of dying. I really needed some air right now.

I heard a sound.

"Nate, is that you?" I asked, hoping it was him.

"No, bitch, it's your worst nightmare." A voice I recognized said.

"Tessa," I said her name. She came into view with several others, they were all Minders, they were all females except for one who was a male. I quickly looked around the forest.

"Are you scared?" A girl asked.

"Of course she is," Tessa said--looking at me. "Meet my family...they hate you for what you did to me."

"What?"

"I can't use my power for three more months, but they can...teach her a lesson." She demanded. Nothing happened for a moment.

"Aah!" I screamed. My whole body was on fire.

"Laurie has a thing for fire," Tessa told me. I started puking. "Sebastian can make anyone puke."

"Stop," I demanded.

"No, I vowed to you that I would make your life miserable." She approached me. "I heard you and Nate got cozy." She kicked me in the ribs. We all heard a crack, it was not from her kicking me, it was me transforming. "Ooh, that had to hurt." A few of my bones began to snap, I was too angry, Tessa kept kicking me.

"STOP!!" I screamed and scratched her with my claws. She screamed.

"Make her puke and burn her even more--" she commanded and they responded.

"Tessa__"

"Two little birds told me that if you transform, there will be no future for you and Nate...I want to speed the process." She kicked me two more times and I snapped. My bones were breaking one by one. I screamed in agony, the pain was too much for me, I wanted to die.

"She's transforming, let's go." Tessa said. I heard them running away, leaving me screaming in agony.

Five minutes letter, the pain stopped. I looked at my hands, they were no longer hands, they were paws, my whole body had fur. I glanced over at my back and saw a tail. I was angry, I was not planning on transforming now or perhaps never.

"A-hoo!!" I howled with anger. I could hear them running in the distance. I could feel their fear. I wanted to make them suffer. I wanted to rip their heads off.

I sprinted after them.

TO BE CONTINUED